another 100 NZ short short stories

another
100 NZ

short short stories

edited by Graeme Lay

First published in New Zealand in 1998 by
TANDEM PRESS
2 Rugby Road, Birkenhead, North Shore City
New Zealand

Introduction and compilation ©1998 Graeme Lay
ISBN 1 877178 26 8

All rights reserved. No part of this publication may be
reproduced, stored in a retrieval system or
transmitted in any form or by any means,
electronic, mechanical, photocopying,
recording or otherwise without prior written
permission from the publishers.

Cover and text design by Sarah Maxey
Typesetting by Egan-Reid Ltd
Copy editing by Jeanette Cook
Printed and bound by Publishing Press Limited, Auckland

Contents

Acknowledgements	9
Introduction	10
LIFE AND TIMES *John McCrystal*	13
NIGHT WATCHES *Wanda Cowley*	15
THE LAST WORD *Victoria Frame*	17
ACAPULCO *Andrew M Bell*	19
DREAM-BABY *Cordelia Lockett*	21
THE HAY PARTY *Diana Menefy*	23
A MERE MARS *Bill Blunt*	25
GUILTY RAIN *Sara Vui-Talitu*	27
FACE VALUE *Janet Peters*	29
POUND DOG *Ellen Shaw*	31
THE WINNING TOUCH *David Hill*	33
BARTHOLOMEW AND THE BEARS *Cherie Barford*	35
NEW TASTES *Adrienne Rewi*	37
AIRPORT CAFE *Kate Barker & Melissa Cassidy*	39
THOUGHTS ON A LIFESTYLE CHANGE SOMEWHERE SOUTH OF HAWERA IN 1862 *Lloyd Jones*	41
THE EYELID *Sheridan Keith*	43
ON THE CHEAP *Simon Robinson*	45
CUSTODY *Linda Burgess*	47
DEAR DIARY *Chris McVeigh*	49
CIVIL OBEDIENCE *Linda Gill*	52
SARAJEVO *Daphne de Jong*	55
THE DOLLS' HOUSE *Kevin Ireland*	57

DEPARTURE TIME *Barry Southam*	59
CITY, COAST, MAN, CHILD *Tina Shaw*	61
KELLY WUZ HERE *Rhonda Bartle*	63
THE MURAL *Graeme Lay*	65
THEY KNOW HOW TO CARE *Jenny Jones*	67
IN MY FATHER'S HOUSE *Jane McKenzie*	69
VIBRATIONS *Catherine Mair*	71
NOW IS THE HOUR *Steve Whitehouse*	73
SEA CHANGE *Julia Oakley*	75
A FOOT IN THE DOOR *Bernard Brown*	77
KNIFE DANCE *Prue Toft*	79
LONDON *Chris Harrison*	81
SMOKE SCREEN *Michael Easther*	82
THE POND *Peter Bland*	83
TESTRIP 100 BUCKS *Virginia Were*	85
GHOST STORY *Elspeth Sandys*	87
FRAMED *Trish Gribben*	89
OVER AND DONE *Kaye Vaughan*	91
WAITING FOR THE TIGER *Rachel Bush*	93
BLUEBOY EXPLORES THE HOTSPOTS *David Lyndon Brown*	95
COFFEE-FRAPPE-COCO *Rachel Buchanan*	97
BONES *Mabel Barry*	99
THE LIFE CLASS *Judy Parker*	101
THE BIRD LADY *Sally Fodie*	102
THE PRISONER *Judith White*	103
THE BLUE TOWEL *Joy MacKenzie*	105
THE CINNAMON GAME *Catherine Chidgey*	107

REAL LIONS *Victoria Feltham*	109
THE BEAUTIFUL LONG BLUE LIBERTY SILK SCARF *Betty Chambers*	111
THAT SUMMER OUT EELING *Rachael King*	113
OBITUARY *Rob O'Neill*	115
THE HOUSE WHERE THE COLLECTOR LIVED *Phill Armstrong*	117
KATIE MORGAN *Tamzin Blair*	119
THE MORALE BOOSTER *Paddy Griffin*	121
BILLY *Gerry Webb*	123
ON A ROLL *Shirley Duke*	125
MY MISTRESS *Neva Clarke McKenna*	127
LAST EXIT *Peter Sinclair*	129
COCKING A SNOOK AT GRAVITY *Patricia Murphy*	131
SHEARING *Jeanette Galpin*	133
MOONLIGHT SONATA *Lianne Darby*	135
FLOWER POWER *Joan Monahan*	137
THE SOUND OF ONE MAN DYING *Tracy Farr*	139
AOTEAROA *R Eastham*	141
FROM THE DEAD LETTER OFfiCE *Olwyn Stewart*	143
THE SMELL OF HORSES *Sue Matthew*	145
CABIN FEVER *Frances Cherry*	147
RUBIES *Toni Quinlan*	149
DOZMARY POOL *Patricia Donnelly*	151
A CLEAN SLATE *Mike Lewis*	153
THE EEL *Anna Gehrke*	155
THE BRIDE *Judy Otto*	157
THE DRAPER'S DAUGHTER *Waiata Dawn Davies*	159
FINAL PEACE *Alison Duffy*	161

NEMESIS *Amelia Wichman*	163
THE KIWI CONTINGENT *Tim Jones*	165
DEVILRIDE *Amanda Clow-Hewer*	167
CONCENTRATION *Denis Edwards*	169
HEAVEN *Nadine LaHatte*	171
SHADOWS *Martha Morseth*	173
A FINE LINE *Louise Wrightson*	175
ARTS PAGE: AN INTERVIEW ABOUT BILL MANHIRE'S WRITING CLASS *Rae Varcoe*	177
JUMPERS *Antonius Papaspiropoulos*	180
ROSES *Tony Chapelle*	183
UNCLE LIONEL TELLS THE TRUTH *Gordon McLauchlan*	185
FROM THE CENTRE OF THE CITY *Diane Brown*	187
SPEECHLESS *Wensley Willcox*	189
DON'T LOOK *Gwenyth Perry*	191
GOING IN *Anita Loni*	193
TOWARDS A SHED AT THE BOTTOM OF THE GARDEN, THE PLUM BLOSSOM SHOWS PINK *Mike Johnson*	195
FANTASY FOR A SUNDAY IN SPRING *Isa Moynihan*	197
STICKING A PIG *Graeme Foster*	199
AFTER HER FATHER (AFTER HER FATHER DIED THE WORLD ...) *Alison Wong*	201
DISAPPEARING ACT *Richard Brooke*	203
WHEN *Frith Williams*	205
IT'S THE HOLES YOU HAVE TO LOOK OUT FOR *Jon Bridges*	207
A GROWTH SITUATION *Joan Rosier-Jones*	209
NEW YEAR'S MOOT *Murray MacLachlan*	211
NOTES ON CONTRIBUTORS	213

Acknowledgements

The editor and publisher would like to thank the following:

Stephen Stratford for his invaluable expertise and advice; Barbara Patterson for her word-processing skills; Rachel Bush and Victoria University Press for their permission to reproduce "Waiting for the Tiger".

Introduction

Readers liked the first ever collection of very short New Zealand fiction. Soon after the publication of *100 New Zealand Short Short Stories*, in May 1997, the book went to the top of the bestseller list. It remained on the list for several weeks, showing that there was a market for what has been called microfiction — stories short enough to read in a few minutes yet satisfying in their content and construction. The literary equivalent of the *Minute Waltz*. Planning for a subsequent edition began a few months after the first collection was published.

This time a competition was launched to attract contributions. It drew over 800 submissions, from all over New Zealand and as far away as London. This inundation presented problems for the editor. When compiling the first collection, it was something of a quest to find 100 quality stories of 500 words or less; for the second there was almost an embarrassment of material. The first collection included some stories which had been published before; with a single exception the second collection consists of previously unpublished work.

Writing a story of publishable quality in only 500 words is a difficult feat, comparable to painting a landscape on a hen's egg, as one observer put it. Setting, characters, conflict, climax and resolution have to be established and contained in about a page and a half of text. Yet the fact that over 800 people rose to the challenge indicated that the art of short short story writing in New Zealand is in good spirits. Many submissions came from people who had been set the task of creating a short short story in writing classes, and the fact that such classes abound throughout the country gives lie to the notion that literacy is undervalued in this country. Many, many people want to be writers. It was particularly heartening to see so many submissions from young writers, and they are well represented in this book. But these are entirely the work of young women. Where have our young male writers gone?

Many people submitted several entries, although quantity proved no guarantee of literary distinction. Yet after the stories had been read and sifted, a significant proportion of the 800 *were* publishable. This sequel could well have been entitled "Another *200* New Zealand Short Short Stories". But 100 it had to be. The top 200 were read, re-read, read again. The final cut was made.

How was this selection carried out? As with all anthologies, editorial preferences and prejudices played their part. There was a predilection for the quirky, the unpredictable, the amusing — writing that showed an awareness of life's absurdities as well as its pain. The writers had also to demonstrate that they were equal to the technical demands of the short short story form.

For fiction of such brevity, the intended effect had to be created in the first sentence. The opening had to be arresting and lead directly into the narrative. The body of the story had to contain an incident or an event of significance and its established circumstances had then to be resolved satisfactorily. Many writers attempted far too much and as a consequence achieved too little. As well, there is such a thing as uncanny coincidence, but it does not play as large a part in our lives as many writers suggested. In many submissions there was also a striving to achieve a surprise ending, but too often this was done at the cost of credibility. Too many twists in the tale and it fell right off.

The chosen 100 short short stories range across the wide and diverse landscape of human experience. There are rural stories, urban stories, outdoor stories, indoor stories, stories from the past and from the future. There are comical stories and melancholy stories and stories drawn from the battle zone between the sexes. Death, or the emotions precipitated by death, is a recurring theme; the trauma of childhood is another. Yet even these serious stories are leavened with a dash of humour.

As with the first collection, many of the best submissions came from new writers. The competition winner was such a writer, John McCrystal. Of his story, "Life and Times", the competition judge, Stephanie Johnson, commented: "It is a beautifully written, moving story which conveys the complexities of a human relationship over many years. It is sad — I was quite tearful at the end — yet it also contains elements of humour." "Life and Times" thus demonstrates the possibilities of the short fiction form and earns its place at the beginning of the book. The stories of second placed entrant Wanda Cowley ("Night Watches") and third placed Victoria Frame ("The Last Word") also possess a quality that sets them apart, even from the other accepted stories. They follow John McCrystal at the front of the collection. The other ninety-seven stories come close behind the winning trio. Highly varied in form and content, they offer a short but satisfying something for everyone.

Graeme Lay

Life and Times
John McCrystal

The first time after the usual manoeuvring — a few films, a couple of dinners, a picnic lunch, a day at the races, many, many drinks, he eager, she reticent — finally in his Austin Princess parked outside her parents' house, each of them at first acutely aware then swiftly oblivious to the groans and creaks of hydrolytic suspension.

The second time very shortly afterward at a West Coast beach, with a buried beer bottle thumbing her hip and her eyes filled with the full moon standing at his straining shoulder, katipo spiders hurrying unsuspected in the marram grass beneath them.

Several times in the Domain, once on the slopes of Mt St John, once on the back seat of the eleven o'clock bus to Glen Innes and once in an unlocked cleaner's cupboard aboard the twin-screw vessel *Hinemoa* en route to Waiheke Island.

Many times in their rented room on Waiheke, a half-full wine bottle on the bedside table, moths fluttering intermittently at the window of the candlelit room like white leaves floating to the surface of dark tea.

On the bonnet of his father's Mercedes-Benz. In every room of her parents' house, including the cleaning cupboard. In the beds of each of his flatmates — they crossed them off a list — while they were out; and, on one thrilling occasion, when a bed-owner was in the kitchen whipping up a banana cake.

Mostly at night; but sometimes during the day, when he could make an excuse at work and she could skip her classes. Sometimes they had picnic breakfast afterward.

Many hundreds of times once they moved into the flat in Grey Lynn, in the queen-size bed he built himself of freshly sawn macrocarpa, the resinous timber redolent of her farmyard childhood, of open fires, of rain in trees, of shade from hot sun, of tankwater.

So often and successfully at first that her sulphur-headed cockatoo began reproducing her climaxes with such remarkable fidelity and equally remarkable bad timing — when they had guests, or when the landlord or their parents called in — that they were forced to throw a blanket over the cage whenever they had company.

After a while, about twice a week, sometimes more, sometimes less.

Once in the same rented room on Waiheke, with candles again, and a half-empty bottle of wine on the bedside table.

Too often, latterly, to pour sweet oil on troubled water, as balm for rawness, as a draught of forgetfulness to erase harsh words, hands on hips, arms folded across breasts.

Once against her will, when he returned drunk after the scene she made when she found the other woman's hairbobble tucked for safe keeping into his pocket where there was also a telltale gram of West Coast sand, and his desperation was greater than her will to resist.

Only once more then, for old times' sake, while his wife was out pushing their youngest in a pram and the other two were downstairs absorbed with *Sonic the Hedgehog*. Afterward, when he was out of the room, she pulled back a corner of the mattress and found there the faint scent of macrocarpa, and she wept for the youth she smelled there, and for the selves and the things and the times that were gone.

Night Watches
Wanda Cowley

The wind's behind us and we're surfing down the south side of the island. The waves we're riding hide the way home. It's exciting and scary. Your brother's on the helm with a sure hand and a silly grin as he looks over his shoulder. Are you surfing in that big cat somewhere on the Indian Ocean? Halfway across, says your last letter from Diego Garcia. Swimming ashore and then seeing the sharks. Twenty years ago you were never allowed into the water until I arrived at the beach, complete with wholesome picnic lunch, first aid kit and beach robes. I remember the day we swam to the reef and I couldn't keep up with the pair of you. That was the first letting go.

We're around the point and the edge is off the wind along this east coast. It's my turn on the helm. We're hyped up and, would you believe it, drinking coffee. Crazy! That's what I thought you were when you took off from Singapore to cross three oceans. Always the one to cause me sleepless nights. To take the long way home. How I used to wish you were like your cousin — domestic, gentle, safe. Not hopping across lava as you climb the son of Krakatoa, dropping your hat into the crater, playing with fire. I remember the day I couldn't hold the helm and the motor was on the blink. You brought us round onto the mooring with panache. That was the second letting go.

This is your first ocean. The chart's on the kitchen wall. The radio is on short-wave weather bands. I sit the watches with you. Dog watch. Graveyard.

Your cousin is in critical care. Your aunt is distraught; full of anger, guilt, questions about drugs and about where she went wrong. I have no answers, only some half remembered lines from Eliot:

The sea howl
and the sea yelp, are different voices
often heard together: the whine in the rigging,
the menace and caress of wave that breaks on water
then something about a tolling bell
older than the time of chronometers, older
than time counted by anxious worried women
lying awake...

 The wind is freshening as we head for the north leg. We take one reef in the sail. And another. The wind screams in the rigging as your brother struggles with the helm. The bloody boat won't point. The swells heave alongside and look down on us. We give up and turn back. It's not an easy option. We're beating into the wind and getting nowhere. I've lined up a tree on the shore and it won't move. Your brother gives in and starts the motor. Everything is geared to carry us forward and we stand still. We lower the main and ride on the storm jib. The tree hasn't moved.

 The tide slacks before the ebb and the wind dies. We inch in towards the shore. The tree moves along the coast and passes us. In control again we head for a sheltered bay. With a sudden gust the wind slams in from the north. There's no way home tonight. Not back, not forward. We get into the dinghy and row to the beach below the farmhouse. Kindly folk, they let us ring your brother's wife and your aunt. Your cousin is off the ventilator and breathing on her own. And you are halfway across your first ocean.

 On the deck I check out the stars. Some of them I know you can see as you chart your course to the Seychelles.

 Rest easy.
 Sail easy.
 Tonight I'm going to sleep.

The Last Word
Victoria Frame

"Imbecile," she whispers to her brother, looking around guiltily in case anybody hears. The expression on his face is stony, but he does not retaliate. She mentally congratulates herself on getting the last word and tries not to chortle out loud.

When they were growing up it was Dean's favourite word. "Imbecile," he would interject if an argument had gone on longer than his liking. She tried calling him the same thing in the beginning, but his reply left her without defence. He knew the meanings of words too thoroughly.

"You are mentally deficient," he would say, "I, on the other hand, have no shortage of brain cells. You are a person of very low intelligence. You are an imbecile." He said this in a quiet undertone while she screeched over the top in objection. He would continue for as long as it took for Kelly to stop protesting. "You are an extremely stupid person," he would conclude, "Therefore there is no question that you are an imbecile."

They were twins, although nobody ever guessed. Dean walked and talked a lot earlier than Kelly; and once trailing, Kelly never seemed to catch up. She was convinced that while in their foetal stage Dean had taken the best of everything, and all that remained for her were the leftovers, remnants.

As she is sitting here with him today, she is reminded of why she has not visited him for two years. It's the awkwardness. Their relationship has not survived into adulthood; it was built on the assumption that they would be children forever. Without the bickering and sniping they have nothing left to say to each other – no common ground.

When they were at home, Dean had an obsession with hedgehogs. He kept them in a large pen on the back lawn. He feared that if he did not capture them they would get run over, and nothing upset him more than a dead animal. He would go out at night with a torch and lure them with bread soaked in milk.

"Don't touch them," warned their mother in the beginning, "or you'll get rabies." But he ignored her, as he so often did, and he never got that particular disease.

Kelly looks on him sadly now, and wonders what might have happened if he hadn't dropped out of school, if – from the beginning – he'd followed a more conservative path. But then she realises with horror that it is this recent attempt to normalise that has killed him – his wife's insistence that he find a secure job, or look for somewhere else to live; his giving up the band scene and becoming an accountant. He died a long time ago. But now people ask: "Why did he do it? His life was finally on track."

"You really are an imbecile," she whispers to him one last time.

"In closing," the minister advises, "I would like to remind you all that there will be a light afternoon tea following the funeral."

How can people eat at funerals? Kelly thinks. All she can think about is decay, the smell of dead hedgehogs.

Acapulco
Andrew M. Bell

Every chance our family got, we'd be off to a surf beach.

Clutching her flutter-board, Mum would kick into a feathering, translucent wall of green, clear enough to see schools of kahawai inside it. Momentarily, all that could be seen were the rubber flowers on her bathing cap as she plummeted with a ton of foam. Then she'd accelerate, squealing with joy, from the white water; like she'd been squeezed from a tube of toothpaste.

Dad used his tall, lean body as a flesh surfboard. With two deft strokes he'd be sliding down the green glass, casually taking a breath before the white water closed over him. It was a point of honour to hold that breath until his nose was nearly in the sand. Even when he'd stopped, he'd lie face down in the water, white hair floating round him like a halo. Then he'd spring up and race out to catch his next wave.

My aunty offered us her bach on the Whangaparaoa Peninsula. Dad could never knock back a free holiday, even if there was no surf there.

At Little Manly beach, Dad's adrenalin went on holiday when he looked at the blue table-top hissing back and forth like a neighbour spilling secrets.

Then he spotted the tawny headland, beckoning him like a Mayan mirage. The pohutukawa anchoring it to the beach were ablaze with Spanish-red flowers, seductive senoritas issuing a challenge. Dad's adrenalin checked in.

"Joan, where are my togs?"

Acapulco. Where bad timing means death or pitiless maiming. I had seen Acapulco in grainy black and white *National Geographic* articles.

Young men, muscled and tanned from hard lives lived outdoors, screwed up their dark, deep-set eyes as they watched the swell hurl itself into that deep fissure in the cliff with a roar like El Diablo. Never flinching as the demon wave sucked back its tongue to expose the wicked teeth that waited to crush them. In, out. In, out. They knew its rhythm like their own heartbeats. Poor but bristling with pride, they relished the chance to test their courage at Acapulco. The need for the tourists' American dollars seemed secondary.

Our Acapulco was not so death-defying, but, far below the clifftop, the surface glinting above the rocks lied about perspective. A knot of the curious gathered, sniggering about "the old guy". My Dad stood, toes up to the edge, a million miles from derision, hearing his own heart in some Mexican heat.

When he sprang, it was as though he'd sucked the sound from their mouths. The world lost its soundtrack as he spiralled into the blue. One somersault. The ocean screaming up to meet him. Half. Running out of sky. Twist. Like a bowstring released. Straighten. Acapulco. Seconds suspended like hours. Acapulco. Peaceful aquariums waiting to smack him into tomorrow. Piercing the water like an arrow. Go shallow. Go shallow. Go shallow.

Dream-baby
Cordelia Lockett

Everybody's dreaming of having babies. First Linda, who really is pregnant so she has an excuse. She gave birth to a Barbie doll. I was dying to know if it moved naturally and just looked like Barbie or was shiny and hard like the real thing. But I thought it might upset her so I just wondered privately. Q. Why doesn't Barbie get pregnant? A. Because Ken comes in another box.

Then there's Andrea. She went to a clairvoyant a few months ago who told her that her soul-mate was a Frenchman. Ever since that she's been desperately saving for a one-way ticket to Paris. I could introduce her to my friend Luc, who's a French chef, but he eats women like bread and washes them down with too much red wine. Andrea's in love with a married man. He says she's part of his life but that he doesn't want an affair. They kiss in bus shelters for hours anyway. She dreamed she had his baby but it was a cat and she hates cats and what do I think that means?

Me. I had a dream that I'd had a baby. Except that it was just a cluster of cells the size of a five cent coin. But that wasn't tragic in itself (don't you love dream-logic?). It had a peculiar way of moving. It would contract its shiny hard body and then sort of flick itself like those black clicky insects you find in the carpet. Actually it was more like one of those frogs that you used to push down and a few seconds later when you turned away would pop up in the air. Like the seal on a jar of bottled pears. I took it on the bus with me, but it kept flicking itself out of my hand and I lost it. So the driver pulled over, and everyone was frantically looking for this thing that looked like a tiny clicking miniature fried egg. Finally someone found it under a bottle top.

Linda came over before to borrow a hammer. She's building a birthing stool (the baby's the wrong way round and she's convinced it's going to be breach). Her midwife, Gaye, recommended she sit on it to try turning the baby. Ages ago Linda was told she only had a quarter of an ovary working and wouldn't be able to conceive, so she didn't bother with contraception and now she's pregnant. Today she had her neighbour's little girl with her who's three or four. And just for a second when she walked in I thought she'd given birth and this was her own child, pre-grown.

My old friend Fran, who has two children, says she dreams about being childless. She says they ruin your life but that she's dying to have another one. She says she misses the smell and that it's a cruel trick played on women by nature.

My boyfriend isn't ready to have a baby yet. The women I know say that men are never ready and that you just have to have one anyway. Then it's an accident. Like a dream.

The Hay Party
Diana Menefy

The last of the hay was in the barn and the gang was celebrating. The older men, eyes bloodshot from weeks of hay dust, watched their sons bash pool balls around the table. An occasional burst of laughter and a crude joke rose above the subdued discussion of the poor season, the low payout and the problems of getting spares for the old Fergie. In the next room the women sat at a table still cluttered with the left-over food, empty plates, wine bottles and beer tops. The talk was of patchwork and books.

Outside, the hills were dark against the grey sky. The drying wind, persistent as ever, whistled around the corners of the house.

Laura leapt up and pulled the heavy drapes across. The phone rang. Her expression changed from annoyance to horror as she listened.

"We're on our way."

"Denise. Her house's on fire," she told the women, then ran to the games room.

"Shut up!" she yelled at the men, then spoke quietly into the stunned silence.

They leapt up, bottles and glasses sent flying, boots mixed up in the scramble for footwear.

"What about the kids?" someone asked.

"I don't know, she didn't say. All she said was it was a big fire."

Vehicles raced in each other's dust. Around the hill the flames could be seen — a deep mass of glowing orange spreading up into black smoke.

The kids were safe. Sitting wrapped in blankets, shivering, out on the lawn. Crying because the house was burning, and Mum was inside, and the puppies were trapped under the verandah.

The men saved a mattress, blankets and a couple of dressing tables before smoke forced them to retreat. Windows exploded. Falling timber fed the shower of sparks. The wind chased the flames into the trees. The roar of the fire was terrifying. There was no water.

The party started up again just after midnight. They sat grouped around the table, the acrid smell of smoke clinging to their clothes, their faces smudged with soot. There were small burns to be treated and glass to be picked out of bare feet — the idiot who never thought to stop and put his boots on. The commercial beer ran out, the home brew was started, the jokes were about fire engines.

The closest had arrived last. The first to arrive couldn't get their pumps to work. All they did was hose down the remains: the chimney, a pile of roofing iron and the burnt-out shells of the washing machine, fridge, bath and freezer. Someone had chopped a hole in the verandah and rescued the dogs. Someone else had been in the hall and heard Denise coughing but couldn't find her in the thick smoke.

And on they talked, but in the end tiredness won. Slowly they left. In groups. No one wanted to go alone. There was comfort in togetherness.

Next morning Laura picked up a plate, broken in the panic, and cried.

A Mere Mars
Bill Blunt

"His loins stirred."

How often have you read that in an old novel? They wrote things like that back then, euphemisms designed to avoid the censor's blue pen and keep the publishers happy. Nowadays you would have no hesitation in writing that he had an erection, or perhaps something even cruder, but of course we now live in more enlightened times. Or so they tell us. Trouble is, women don't, do they? Or at least my Wendy doesn't. If my loins stir she says "Stop it!" I mean, I ask you. As if there was any choice in the matter. It's like telling a bloke with chronic eczema not to scratch or a woman with acute migraines to stop having a headache.

"I can't help it," I tell her. "It's just natural."

"Well you seem to have one all the time," she says. "Don't."

"I'm sorry," I say, and try a bit of psycho-flattery. "It's being near you all the time. You bring me on." Which is hardly a lie. Wendy is good to look at, with all the gym work she does and the clothes she buys that fit her like a second skin which she insists on taking off in front of me when we're getting ready for bed. Am I supposed to look the other way? Ignore the black hip highs and the lacy bits?

"Wendy. I'm twenty-four," I said to her once. "We've been married a year. What's it going to be like when we're forty?"

"Don't even mention it!" she said with so much finality that I dropped the subject immediately. Now I'm a fixit sort of bloke. When I see a problem looming I like to fix it quickly, that's why I'm getting on so well at work. They tell me I have foresight and I'm an ace at problem solving. So I think to myself, Wendy, here's a potential problem and I'm going to solve it before it becomes serious.

So I'm going down to the library and I get out all those books that are now the rage and start boning up on relationship development techniques and similar trendy ideas. All those Venus and Mars things, Masters and Johnson, Shere Hite, and volumes about erroneous zones and feelgoodness. It took me a month to get through them but I felt prepared. Mr Fixit is ready.

"Wendy, can we talk?"

"OK," she says, "but make it quick, there's a Brad Pitt movie coming on. He's gorgeous!"

So I expound my new-found knowledge, explaining all the nuances of modern thinking about the war of the sexes. How there must be understanding and acceptance of the differences on each partner's part and how there doesn't need to be conflict and the battle lines really don't exist. I thought I was good. She doesn't hear a word.

"OK," she says. "So? All this explains what?"

"Why," I say weakly, "when I'm around you I get randy."

"Well don't," she says.

Guilty Rain
Sara Vui-Talitu

I can't I can, thought Sina. *Wrestling with her indecision she gazed at the white wall in front of her and sighed.* She shared the hospital waiting room with a palagi woman who appeared strangely more relaxed, although she avoided Sina's curious stares. Sina felt the knots in her stomach tighten with the uncertainty of her decision. Posters on the noticeboard spoke of life rather than death. She picked up a magazine and flicked through it. The pictures showed happy families, but Sina knew her family would be far from happy if they knew the secret embedded in the depths of her soul.

At school she had shown academic promise as an all-rounder before the most popular senior boy had chosen her. He was so nice and caring, with big brown eyes only for her – Sina from Samoa. He had been her first, and she had thought it would last forever like in the movies. She had dreamed of a big traditional church wedding with five bridesmaids and as many guests as could fit into the church hall. Her mother had always warned her about the evils of men, but only now she understood. It was barely a month when the tide changed and he stopped calling. He left school and the rumour was he had joined the Caleb gang down south.

Sina never felt more alone in her silent dilemma. No one knew she was with child. God forgive me, she thought. Disguised with her cap pulled low and dark sunglasses, she hoped no one would recognise her. Outside, the bright sun was in contrast with her dark inner turmoil. Life in New Zealand was more pressured than in the Islands. Most girls her age had given birth, most outside of marriage. But everyone would know, fingers would point and silent whispers would run like the wind.

The minutes seemed to drag slowly forward counting down her doom. Sina's voices in her head began to speak. Faster and faster. Louder and louder. "Ms Crae?" called the nurse. Sina breathed a sigh of temporary relief. Sina watched her go and knew she was next. The walls seemed chokingly claustrophobic and her breathing grew short and sharp. She felt sick, remembering her best friend Tila who had wrapped her baby in plastic and thrown it in the trash before committing suicide a week later. Sina's pastor father had a reputation to protect and she was certainly doomed to a fate worse than death if they knew. But this would be Sina's secret for life. Tears filled her eyes.

The sound of footsteps became louder. "Ms Tui?" called the nurse. Sina froze, then slowly stood up. She glanced out the window at the rain.

Twenty minutes later Sina emerged. The rain reminded her that God was crying for her baby as her own tears fell on the lino.

Face Value
Janet Peters

Hart emanated rebellion. She'd chosen both her name and her attitude. Everything was pierced: lips, nose, eyebrows and ears sported silver rings. Tiny rings were tortured into complex arrangements as tight as the pearls around her mother's neck. Strategic rips decorated her black tunic and tights. There were even silver rings pierced into the woven tunic fabric.

The scuffed Doc Martins, seemingly oversize, were planted firmly on the ground. "Don't mess with me!" her stance said. But then, temporarily forgetting her attitude, one spindly leg bent and the leather-clad toes rubbed an itchy spot on her calf transforming her into the child that she still was.

People moved forward slightly.

At first Hart resisted, because that was what she was wont to do. Resist, desist, disagree. The point made to her satisfaction, she, too, inched forward. She caught a couple of women looking at her. "Bugger them, let them look," she said to herself. Look at *them*. Her jaw jutted. How pathetic. She stared defiantly at the women and immediately they both glanced away. Hart's partially shaven head with its red Mohawk brush quivered in increasing outrage. Why the hell are they here? Look at them — Remuera tarts. What would they know? It's obvious they've never had to worry about money for a start. God, their clothes alone are worth more than a year's dole! She glared again at the women who were by now both steadfastly focusing on objects in the distance. Pleased at the effect of her actions, Hart's anger subsided.

A few steps forward again.

She was jostled slightly from behind. Hart turned sharply, ready to defend her territory. "Sorry," the woman beside her said, quickly sensing her mistake. Hart gave her the eye and increased the distance between them. And look at her, what's she doing here? A mouse, that's what she looks like. Brown hair, brown clothes, pale, freckled skin. Hart smirked to herself as she completed her vision of the woman nibbling a hunk of cheese. I bet she's got nothing better to do. Probably hasn't got a life. She's just come here for a bit of action.

People moved again.

Laughter from a group of three men broke into her reverie. Immediately thinking they were laughing at her, she glared at them. But no, a private joke was being shared. And them? What brought these three here? Hart watched them. Suits, that's what they are. She tried to figure out their relationship. Gay? Hart looked for a flirtatious look, a light touch on the arm. But no. As the men continued to chat she viewed them closely. Brothers? Guys who work together? Fuck, who cares? Bored now, Hart turned her attention away.

Shuffle, shuffle. A few more inches were gained.

The fragrance of daphne and freesias was filling the air. Flowers were strewn on either side of the path. Hart closed her eyes. She'd always had a secret weakness for flowers. Not that anyone would ever know. God, the first and only time Mick brought her flowers she was enraged! Flowers were for hippies. Punks were staunch! She closed her eyes and momentarily forgetting her public persona, breathed deeply, revelling in the scent. Ooh, nice.

The last few steps.

Hart took a deep breath. She'd never been good around grief. Her hands tightened around the single, perfect, pale pink camellia she was holding. She held the flower out and placed it under the photo. She stared at the open book and reached for the pen. "Goodbye, Queen of Hearts," she wrote.

Pound Dog
Ellen Shaw

The woman always walked her dog on the beach.
Except when the tide was in and then they went elsewhere for a week. Walking kept the woman fit. She was proud of her strong legs, the lack of fat on them, even though the rest of her body was a bit weighty.

The dog gambolled and played and ran. She was a medium-sized, muscular animal and delighted in throwing pinecones into the air or rolling them down slopes, dancing along behind, her mouth open as if laughing, her eyes intent. Sometimes she'd leap into the air and turn a full circle before coming down again. The dog woofed for joy while pulling at logs, or running on the stone-strewn beach, splashing in the water. The woman loved watching her. She'd stop and feast on the creature's delectation, proud here too, for a year ago the creature had been just a pound dog, one day away from being killed, and when the woman took her home, she shivered and shook at leaves falling, wind blowing, the sea moving and cringed when the woman spoke to her. The dog was young and the woman nearly old, but they suited each other.

Their beach was lonely, inhospitable to picnickers and sunbathers with its oyster-shell and rock-covered shore, its muddy, tidal waters. Only walkers came and the occasional shell-pickers, so when the woman was found, she'd been dead for a few hours and baptised in her dying as never in her living by the creeping low tide which anointed her sweetly, then left.

Did she fall or was she pushed? the police wondered. The front of her head smashed into a rock certainly. That and the water killed her, but her legs in her shorts showed abrasions behind and above the knees. As if she'd been given a bit of a blow in that area on both upper legs. But there was no weapon, nothing heavy around. The sea had been and gone of course, a gentle swabber, no carrying strength, kind to her. And she was getting on, sixty seven wasn't it? She could have tripped on a stone or slipped in the mud. Might have hurt her legs earlier sitting on the oyster-shells. Odd though to sit on oyster shells. Still they called it misadventure.

Two friends took the dog. She was such a pretty, friendly little thing. They walked her occasionally on the same beach, although they preferred the next one along which was sandy with plenty of people. The dog, however, liked the rocky place, more to do, cones to find, logs to pull up and run with. My God, she's strong said the couple, and how she can go. Look at her with that huge branch. A bash from that and you'd know it!

The dog rang swiftly and easily towards them, but when she was told to Stop! No! Good girl! Stay! she did almost at once and dropped her log. Then she sat, swishing her tail back and forth, back and forth in the mud, smiling a happy-dog smile.

The Winning Touch
David Hill

They meet at "their" café. He has it planned. She has it planned.

Since last Sunday's movie, the anticipation is there whenever they meet. They meet constantly now. They are quickened by each other's presence.

Today, when he sees her sitting at just the right table, anticipation almost reaches the visible spectrum.

It crystallised during the movie. It was so corny that they were both looking forward to laughing about it. The hero reaching out one hand, the heroine turning her head as his fingertips grazed her cheekbone, her cheek nestling into the hero's palm. Both of them knew instantly that this would be them.

They haven't said so – of course. They chuckled at the scene when they discussed the movie afterwards. They discuss everything; they delight in each other's liveliness.

She smiles as he approaches the table. Her face brightens. He feels his own eyes crinkle.

They already know they will be a long-term thing. It's the second time round for them both, and they want it to be the best. Each moment must be as perfect as possible.

That includes the moment about to come. Within the next half hour, they will touch each other.

They've already touched formally. She took his hand the night they met at a friend's dinner party. He's taken her arm as they crossed the street, and felt her position the arm in a way which showed that she welcomed his gesture.

"Hi, how are you?" he says now, as he sits.

"I'm fine. How are you?" She smiles again. She likes his voice. He likes her smile. They like everything about each other.

And now they are moving towards this first unequivocal touch. It will define their later lives; it must be done well. No lunges, collisions, bumping of foreheads; this moment is to be well, sacramental.

Everything goes right. The café owner passes and greets them by name. The coffee is at its best. The other patrons are few and decently focused elsewhere. Lighting and room temperature are at optimum.

"There's a chamber concert the Saturday after next," he tells her.

"Shall we go?" she says immediately. She likes him so much, and it's not fair that he should do all the work.

They smile at each other. They hold each other's eyes. The time (and the timing) are perfect. His hand, he is pleased to note after a surreptitious wipe on his jeans, is dry. Her cheek, she is glad to see after a discreet glance in the wall mirror, is unblemished.

He reaches across the table. His fingertips graze her cheekbone.

The touch electrifies them. Healthy flesh on both sides has been without this for too long. Pulses, electric shocks, lightning bolts shoot between them.

She catches her breath, and turns her head faster than intended. He holds his breath, and moves his hand faster than intended.

And as her head turns and his hand moves, his right index finger slides neatly into her left nostril.

Bartholomew and the Bears
Cherie Barford

Bartholomew Pike took to wearing bare feet when the polar bears turned green at the zoo. He heard about it on his Walkman one sunny morning on the 8 am bus. The driver laughed at his concern.

"Happens to genuine blondes every summer mate. Specially in public swimming pools. Something to do with chemicals an' sun an' water not mixin' right. Turns hair mouldy."

Bartholomew felt uneasy. He'd only encountered green bears in animal biscuit packets at children's parties.

"Do you think there's pink elephants and purple tigers out there?"

The driver shook his head. "Not likely. Chlorinated water turns blondes green, not pink or purple. Anyway, autumn's almost here, an' it only happens in summer."

"Well," said Bartholomew, "someone has to do something." He removed his footwear and threw it out the window. "Bears forever! May they find their true selves!"

The 8 am bus hooted and whistled all the way to town. Bartholomew sat quietly in his business suit, briefcase beside him. "Something's very wrong with this world, driver," he said as he stepped off the bus.

The driver thought he looked silly standing on the footpath with bare feet. "You can't cry for the whole world, mate."

Bartholomew stared at him. "I never cry, driver. When I'm sad, I just imagine I'm somewhere else."

The company boss thought Bartholomew's feet were a joke. "Your toes, Pike," she laughed. "They're all scrunched up. Didn't you ever run around in bare feet as a child?"

"It's the bears," he cried, two weeks later when she asked him what was wrong. "They're still green."

She faxed headquarters: "Still no shoes. I think his wife's left him."

"Warn him about athlete's foot," came the reply.

Bartholomew left the office. He disliked the static from the nylon-blend carpet, and the fake flowers on his desk. He took to roaming the city. Slept rough. People compared him to Saint Francis because he wandered parks with pigeons and people on crutches. It was said that on cold nights his lips turned bluer than his feet.

Street kids befriended him. They gave Bartholomew a pair of boots which he hung around his neck and promised to wear when the polar bears smiled.

"Reckon they'll smile if we dance for them?"

"No," Bartholomew replied. "Green bears can't smile."

One extra-cold night, Bartholomew tried to warm himself in a local café, but wasn't allowed in. "I like your tie," management explained. "Your coat's fetching, your trousers well-made; but we have a dress code: no shoes, no food."

Bartholomew turned slowly away. He was never seen on the streets again.

The 8 am bus heard that he was found swimming naked with the polar bears at the zoo. "Kept asking the police for his boots," said the driver. "Blue all over an' all he wanted was his boots."

The 8 am bus hooted and hollered all the way to town.

New Tastes
Adrienne Rewi

She was 15 and a virgin. He was 37 and married, and he had a case full of ripe mangoes.

The light was dim in the small cabin and the heavy scent of ripe tropical fruit hung in the air. They were sailing between Samoa and Fiji and she was pleased that no-one had seen them slip down the narrow steel ladders into the bowels of the ship. She knew she shouldn't have been there, but she was drawn by a powerful urge that she couldn't explain. His dark eyes had offered her excitement and mystery and she was ripe for adventure.

In the half-light she saw the case of perfectly packed fruit and she was drawn by their exotic smell.

"What are these?" she asked in innocence.

"Mangoes," he replied, behind her.

She ran her hands across the fat, fleshy fruit and wondered what they would be like to eat. Their leathery green and gold skins glowed and she wanted to squeeze their plumpness between her fingers. But he'd taken the fruit from her and had started undressing her. His tongue prowled around her neck and his kisses made her weak. She suddenly felt out of her depth and as he lowered her down onto the narrow bunk, she had a sudden urge to count the mangoes. She drew in the smells that encircled her and she wondered what sort of tree mangoes grew on.

His tongue was between her legs and she didn't know why. Then his full brown lips smothered hers with a strange new taste. He entered her and she cried out. He wiped her eyes with his tongue and he said it would be all right.

Afterwards he peeled her a mango and the juice ran down his wrists.

"Is this the first time you've tasted mangoes?" he asked.

She nodded. It was an indescribable flavour and she liked it. He cut off a long, slippery slice of fruit and as he placed it between his lips, he kissed her again letting their juices mingle with the sweet fruit. He licked her chin free of rivulets of yellow syrup. "If you visit me again, you can have another one," he said.

She nodded again and wondered how long the fruit would take to ripen properly.

Airport Café
Kate Barker & Melissa Cassidy

The airport café clock reads 11.55 pm.

Intellectual Yanks lounge in baseball caps and leather executive everything. Their table is strewn with dead food cartons, envelopes and gold-plated pens. They lean back and philosophise, crunching their post-softdrink ice.

Three tables down, two women pool together for a cup of iced water to wash down their two-day-old farmbaked cookies. Necessity has forced surrender to the rampant demands of consumerism. They carefully clear their table before vacating the scene of the crime.

The scuttling women are hardly noticed by the unshaven long-hair drinking alone. He has two handles of beer; does he think this makes him look less conspicuous, or is he simply waiting for companionship? Perhaps his responsible and judgmental son? His jetsetting, bankrupting wife? Or his long-distance mistress, maybe.

As the lone woman absently ponders the man's motives, her plastic spoon breaks on the half-eaten cheesecake. Her new 1.8 litre Toyota sits in the carpark holding just enough gas to get home. Money is tight, she can't make the escape she desires. People-watching at the airport café is enough compromise for now. She notices the uniforms and begins a new chapter in observation.

Two flight attendants collapse into a stolen moment's peace between shifts. They feel briefly human again; discuss their wives left home in the real world with babies, daytime television, phone gossip and credit cards. The wives look after the money, but they know how to spend it too.

The frugal women eye the bookshop, nibbling their cookies. They choose, consider, ignore. Something else, consider, pass it over. They dare to linger, touch, caress, then ultimately curb their flirting over unobtainable goods and move on.

Security wonders briefly if the two browsing women are shoplifters. His muscle-bound arms are magnetically propelled from his shoulders, he oozes bully-boy training and God help anyone who looks as furtive as he does. His girlfriend coos that he looks like Bruce Willis — so did his last girlfriend. He watches a lot of Bruce Willis movies. Always alone.

A casual suit ambles by the guard, vaguely self-conscious. The most radical thing he's ever done is let his hair grow long. It's not fashionably long, but wavy black, almost permed. He's overweight and his nearly-permed radical hair doesn't suit him. Nobody laughs though — he is six foot five — and BIG.

Everybody here is connected by waiting. Waiting to leave, waiting to serve, waiting to consume, waiting for the next plane. I've been waiting for some time. I'm tired. But there's nowhere else to wait. This is where I was waiting when her flight exploded onto the tarmac.

"Calling emergency services," they said. "Wait here."

"Checking the wreckage," they said. "Wait here."

"No survivors," they said. "Wait here."

I wait here. No one comes.

I'm tired of waiting. But it won't be much longer.

The airport café clock reads 11.59 pm.

The explosives are set for midnight.

Thoughts on a Lifestyle Change Somewhere South of Hawera in 1862
Lloyd Jones

We were hacking and slashing. Sweat poured out of ripped uniforms. Keats wore a big face wound. Half his lip was torn away. He was a bulging mess of injury and pride.

Presently we came to a clearing. A clear water stream trundled down to a beach where the sea heaved up and withdrew again. Keats and the lieutenant dipped their bloody faces in the stream. I took off my boots and walked across the piping hot sand. My feet were red as liver and the salt water rushed about my toes. I looked northwards in the direction of the dirty brown smoke colonnading up to the puffy skies where we had driven out the local population. Our company had split according to their dispersal, with me and Keats and the lieutenant playing cat and mouse with a party of resistance along the coast.

There was a nice shelf set back from the beach. Dark with solemn timber and ground fern. I was thinking to use all the timber I cleared. I'd build a bach, dig a vegetable patch and grow my tobacco. I suddenly realised I could probably use a smoking hut as well, and a fence, and as I compiled my list of "necessaries" the line of the forest receded. I began to see in there a farming possibility.

At dusk we lashed together a raft of ponga trunks. The lieutenant sent me off to find a long stick and a heavy stone. We pushed off from shore. Keats in his shirt sleeves cleaning his musket, while I felt for the ocean floor with the end of the manuka pole, pushing us further out to safety till we dropped anchor.

All night the bush cooed and shook and hooted. Keats said it was the Maoris interrogating the forest for our whereabouts; and in the dark we smiled at our cunning. "Story time," said the lieutenant, and

Keats finished up last night's story about Odysseus escaping the Cyclops' cave by tying himself to the belly of a sheep. We nodded contentedly after that.

Daybreak. I shoved our party ashore. We found a trail of footprints across the beach. The party had passed here in the night right under our floating noses.

I was happy about that. I was getting sick and tired of all the killing, even though the lieutenant was open-mouthed at what had got away and was looking left and right up the beach. To compensate, he fired up to the treetops and dropped a pigeon from its crow's nest.

I prepared it and spit-roasted it while the lieutenant sat on a log writing in his diary and Keats, with thought to writing to his brother, Freddy, held a leaf of letter writing paper to his knee. *May 1*. He got that down and then looked up with contentment at the generous treetops and the spreading skies, and that torn lip and one tooth coagulated into the single thought that this was the life, dear Freddy. This was the time of our lives.

The Eyelid
Sheridan Keith

May I tell you something? When I was a child I thought I had only the one eyelid, that it stretched above my eyes like the roof of the verandah. I made it go up and down. It was only later, when I learnt to wink, that I realised there were two. Where did I go when I closed the lid? My mother said I went to Dreamland.

When I went to school the teacher pulled down a map. Most of the time it was furled into a tight roll above the blackboard. He pulled it right down, but sometimes it would snap away, taking Africa and America back into its dark curl. He pointed to New Zealand using a wooden pointer. That was where we lived, down there, in that blue part called The Pacific Ocean.

I walked home from school alone, looking into people's gardens, thinking about their fences. Some had wooden fences with sharp points, some had stone walls you could walk on, sometimes there were hedges so tall I couldn't see over them. Then there were those fences made out of wooden posts with strands of tight wire forever waiting to burst apart.

I met my husband at a dance. I was sitting on a bench looking down at my feet. I saw him coming towards me, but perhaps he would ask Sally, sitting next to me. But his feet stopped exactly in front of mine. I remember the black polished toes of his shoes and the way they stopped exactly opposite my white strappy sandals. We danced together, and the hand he placed at the back of my waist felt tender but strong.

We were married in a church built of stone. The steeple pointed into a sky that was blue with strands of white cloud more beautiful than my dress. I said, the clouds are more beautiful than my dress. My husband replied, but not as beautiful as your hair.

Our house had a lily pond in the garden. The water tried to reflect the sky, but the leaves of the lilies were lush. There were shy goldfish. I grew vegetables in rows and beans up a frame. I planted a daphne bush right next to the front steps so that he would smell it as he brushed past coming home from work. We had two children, a boy and a girl.

After my husband died, they brought me here. There is a garden, but no lily pond. There is a hedge in the front, but the people here don't tell me where I am, only that I must not wander away. Where would I wander to?

At night I close my eyelid really tight. I dance with my husband. The music is slow. He is wearing his ming blue tie, and his black shoes gleam. I ask him where we are, but he only ever says, keep dancing, darling. We must all keep dancing.

On the Cheap
Simon Robinson

People don't like to spend thousands on burying relatives, Dave thought. Bloody hell, he couldn't think of anyone in his family whose burial he would pay for. Or cremation. Well, his mum, sure. But not his father. Nor his brothers. Uncle Jack, perhaps Nah, bugger him. He was a funny old bloke, but what had he ever done for Dave?

The idea grew. Dave was full of plans to make millions. And this was a cracker. He called Jeff: "I've got an idea."

"What?"

"Budget funerals. Most places charge thousands. We'll do em cheap."

Dave dug around in the bottom of the bedroom cupboard, found his older brother's rusty roof racks, attached them to Jeff's purple Mazda. He placed an ad in the local paper and bribed the butcher to put a poster in his window. And the barber, but he would only hang it inside. "It'll scare people off in the window," the barber said.

Their first customer rang eleven days later. It was Sarah from the other side of town. Her mum had died and, "Well," said Sarah, who was on the dole, "I can't afford anything too flash." Dave and Jeff were there within an hour. Dave had bought six plywood coffins from a mate's mate in Auckland. Normally they came with a veneer, but they were cheaper raw.

" G'day," said Jeff as Sarah appeared at the door, red eyed, wet haired.

"Yeah, g'day. We're sorry to hear about your mum."

Sarah stared out at the car. The coffin rested across the roof racks, held on by three bungee cords which Jeff had stolen from a neighbour. "Budget Funerals," read the sign in the back window. Dave had forgotten to hide it.

"Don't you have to have a special licence, or something?" Sarah asked.

"Don't think so," said Dave. "We'll just take her down to the cemetery. I think you just sort of drop them off. We can ring the priest if you want."

Sarah looked worried. "I think you're meant to leave them for a few days. Dana's coming home tomorrow, we should wait until then."

Dave frowned. "OK," he said. "What about if we leave the coffin here till tomorrow afternoon? No later. We've got a business to run."

That was the best idea, Sarah said, and together they carefully lifted the body into the coffin.

"This is going to be easy," Dave said as the two boys drove off down the road whooping with excitement at their first business. "People are always dying."

They didn't see the truck hurtling toward the one lane bridge over Rangiwhaia creek. The collision snapped the bridge in half and the twisted purple Mazda bounced into the water. It took the fire brigade four hours to drag the bodies out. Internal injuries, they pronounced solemnly. Internal injuries.

Across town Sarah was combing her mother's grey hair and applying red lipstick to her thin blue lips.

Custody
Linda Burgess

I stayed at his place on Thursday and Friday nights, so things are looking up. We really *have* been getting on. Then on Saturday it was his turn to walk the dogs — I've told you about that, haven't I? You know, when he broke up with Anna and all that, and she bought his share of the property, they sort of kept joint custody of the dogs. I know, hilarious, isn't it. So every second Saturday he goes round to walk them. Well, he took me too, so I saw that as a good sign.

Well. Anyway. When we got round there, Brian, her new bloke — in fact I think he's bought Roger's share of the house — he was there. They're making real settling down noises.

They both knew what time Roger was coming to pick up the dogs, and there was Brian sitting on the sofa taking a break from painting. I looked at Roger and I could see what he was thinking: *his exes* — ex-wife, ex-dogs, ex-house, and there's this new guy painting it. It's like tagging, isn't it. *Isn't* it? Well I think, and Roger does too — I know he does though he hasn't said as much — that Anna and Brian are going to try for a baby.

Roger never wanted a baby.

So it was all very civilised and Brian even got out a bottle of something, a pretty decent chardonnay actually, and that pissed Roger off because he knows his wines. Well, there we were sitting and drinking, and I was getting on well with Anna. *Very.* No, I don't think she's jealous. Hard to tell. She's busy looking happy to be with Brian — happy *plus*, because she knows Roger still cares. Well he does. He does. Getting over it, but he does. And Brian and Roger are sitting on the sofa, side by side, and what I start to notice — and honestly, I could have laughed it was so funny, but of course you don't, one doesn't, I didn't — but what I noticed was they were doing mirrored body language. You know, Brian would lean back with his hands behind his head, so Roger would too; then Roger crossed his legs, and so on.

God it was *so obvious*.

Well, on the way home, I told Roger that. He didn't say anything, so I told him sometimes it was him copying Brian, and sometimes Brian copying him. I said it just went to show. And I said I wondered what Anna was thinking, and the fact that Brian was painting the spare room did look like they were thinking of having a baby. Didn't it?

Things had been going so well that I thought I'd stay over at his place again on the Saturday night. One of these days he might even stay at mine. What? No. He didn't. And I didn't. He dropped me off. Not sure why? But there's always next weekend.

I suppose.

Dear Diary
Chris McVeigh

Monday October 27

Time to break out and show my real identity. Bought myself some Reeboks and a skateboard, then took off. Must admit, though, I looked a bit of a fool when the rollers caught on the edge of the lift well and I fell head-first into the office reception area. Jane Fromont from Audit was passing at the time and wasn't impressed. Shame, really, I rather fancy her.

Thursday November 1

Got on the Internet today. My new Pentium Discovery 545 is great fun. Haven't really mastered the mouse yet. Supposed to be "getting on-line" (that's the expression we use) with a firm in Prague to discuss new solvency data but ended up getting a message from a man in Dayton Ohio who wants to s*ck my c**k. How disgusting.

Wednesday November 9

To the theatre with Angela from Human Resources. Quite a nice meal first at Beppis. Angela had something called cannelloni (she's spent some time in Greece, I think), I decided to play it safe and opted for what the waiter described as steak and fried bread. Since when has pâté and bone marrow been served with porterhouse?

The play was better. Hedda's Gobbler, I think it was called. I've always enjoyed Ibsen, even though I can't pretend to understand that dense Scandinavian symbolism. I fell asleep during Act II, unfortunately.

Thursday November 17

Mother phoned. She's always had this rather annoying ability to manage me with politeness. "Would you be an angel and pick up my dry-cleaning?" means *"Do it now!"* So I did, as always. Two duvet covers and an article of transparent blue lingerie. What *does* mother get up to? Decided to go to the movies, then changed my mind and mowed the lawn instead. Love being close to nature. I have a hole in my sock.

Friday November 25

The end of the week, thank goodness. As usual the partners and associates (not the staff) had a quiet drink on the eighth floor. Heard some political Wally say that he's had a bilateral discussion. What on earth does he mean? Is the English language slipping me by? The senior partner is retiring (well, he's actually quite outgoing, but you know what I mean). This might mean an opportunity for me except that Roger D. from Management has a double degree and they want some legal clout. I headed him off socially though, by adding some tonic to the office manager's single malt. I've always been a good mixer.

Saturday December 3

Off to spend the weekend with my friends the Healeys at their beach in the Sounds. Must have got the date wrong as, when I arrived, the place was deserted. Either that or they changed their minds. Would've rung them, but I don't have a cell phone and I didn't have enough change for the call box. Should I buy a cell phone? The firm won't pay unless you're a partner. Once took the plunge and bought a mail-order carphone. Slightly miffed when I received a phone in the shape of a Ford Prefect. Sent it back, but they'd already charged my credit card.

Lost a filling when biting on a hamburger.

Sunday December 4

Decided to go to the gym. Noticed some unsightly cellulitis on my left leg. There's also the two-tone lycra body suit I won in the Christmas raffle. Not sure if heliotrope's my colour, though. Then came home and had a lie down. Stared at the ceiling for a while and read a few more pages of Grisham's latest. Work again tomorrow.

What am I going to do with my life? Some say it's never too late to reinvent yourself, but I'm not so sure. I'm not even sure I know what that means. What about something totally nouveau, like a stud in my ear?

Must plant my scarlet runners this week.

Mother rang again.

Civil Obedience
Linda Gill

Emily Cochrane stood in front of the yellow bottle bank which lay like a wrecked ship, listing and rusting, on the lawn in front of the church. The porthole openings above her head were labelled "Green," "Brown," "Clear," with the stern authority of traffic lights. She had been about to put her first bottle into the "green" hole, but as she was lifting it, the light had shone through and it looked brownish. So now she was looking at the bottle again, holding it up to the light, lowering it to waist level, trying to decide whether it was brownish green or greenish brown.

The ground around her feet was littered with glass shards and crinkle-edged bottle tops. A pile of partly squashed cardboard cartons waited soggily for new owners and a new life. Taggers had covered the sides of the banks with their hieroglyphs, and Emily Cochrane found herself as usual trying to make sense of them.

Brown or green? A decision had to be made, even if arbitrarily. She reached up, dropped the bottle into the "green" hole and winced when it smashed in the steel vault. The chilling, thrilling sound shattered the stillness of the quiet street.

Emily glanced apologetically at the front window of the houses around her and then at the sixteen large cartons she had lined up in front of the bottle bank. She bent down and pulled out a clear bottle, stepped sideways to the appropriate hole, stood on tiptoe so that her hand would reach as far as possible into the bank and let go. The bottle smashed as resoundingly as the first.

Hope you're all at work, Emily said to the house fronts. And began. She danced from hole to hole, orchestrating the colour-coded percussive rhythm. Three greens – smash, smash, smash. Pause. Two clear – smash,

smash. One brown (a beer bottle, no hesitation here). Green, brown-green but I'll call it green. She worked more quickly — clear clear brown clear, green green, brown, green, brown.

Her attention was distracted by a piece of paper pinned onto the worn noticeboard that announced the name of the church and the times of services. She stopped dropping bottles for a moment and walked over to read it.

When you are walking with your doggie
And it does a doggie do
Remember who it belongs to
And take it home with you

On the other side of the noticeboard there was a plastic bag containing a Doggie Pooper Scooper and a hand-written note that these were available within.

If you take your doggie for a walk
Green, green, clear…

The words sang in Emily Cochrane's head, fitting rhythmically with her resumed bottle-dance.

And it does heap of shit (brown)
Please buy a Pooper Scooper
And chuck it round the town
If your doggie does a green do
And you think it should be brown

Oh help, thought Emily Cochrane, I've just put a brown bottle in the "green" hole. She looked up at the three openings, calculated to be of a height and size to prevent anyone from retrieving a bottle once it was inside.

Oh what the hell. She flung herself on the remaining bottles, green, brown and clear, and crammed them as fast as she could, two or three at a time into the "brown" hole — most colours when mixed up turned brownish, she remembered from her oil-painting days. At the bottom of the last carton lay a small blue bottle. Emily stood well back and threw it hard and accurately into the "clear" opening. Now, she thought, the clear glass will have a lovely bluish tinge, like putting Reckitts' Blue with the whites. Her mother used to do this.

She jumped on her cartons, added them to the damp pile beside the bottle bank and got back into her car. It had been an exhilarating morning.

Sarajevo
Daphne de Jong

I remember years ago, an afternoon tea party given by the Mother's Union or the Red Cross — some group like that. A Yugoslavian woman with greying black hair and snapping black eyes told us how during the war she and some other girls from her village used to go out at night during the Occupation and cut the German telephone wires. She told it matter of factly, with a hint of glee. Her husband, who was her fiancé then and who now worked in the local dairy factory and joked in broken English with his mates, was fighting up in the hills, and these girls used to go out at night and cut the wires and roll them up and hide them in the woods.

Everyone had stopped sipping their tea and the little Yugoslav woman blushed, seeing they were all listening. "How old were you?" someone asked.

"Seventeen. We were all sixteen, seventeen, eighteen."

"What if you'd been caught?"

She giggled. There was a gap between her front teeth, which were just slightly too prominent, but you could see she must have been pretty at seventeen or eighteen. "Shot." She said it merrily. "They would shoot us." And she turned to her youngest grandchild who was pulling at her skirt, asking for a biscuit. She put the child on her knee and bent her head over its black curls. And we began talking about something else.

There was a picture in the paper yesterday of a teenage girl lying on the street in Sarajevo, her body riddled with bullets.

I remember that woman sitting there in her ordinary cheap dress with her ordinary, sunbrowned face, and the skin around her eyes wrinkling as she laughed.

I wondered, when her children were growing up, had she told them the story of how she used to sneak out at night and roll up the German telephone wires when she was their age? Of what she did for her country.

The Dolls' House
Kevin Ireland

Morton Black's great delight in life was his doll collection. He owned almost two hundred species. Most sat around his living room, on shelves and sofas and chairs. But the best of them, the truly prize dolls, gazed down adoringly at him from the top of a wardrobe in his bedroom.

Some were modern, but most he had chanced on in second-hand shops. Several were old and valuable. They came from all around the world and included bridal dolls, milkmaids, fairytale characters, ballerinas, princesses and dolls in ethnic costumes. The one feature they shared was that all were women.

Morton had not set out deliberately to gather females about himself. What happened was that, as the collection grew, he discovered he was specialising. Almost everyone who collects anything, from postage stamps to porcelain, has probably gone through the same experience. Female dolls arrived in his life through sheer good fortune. It was as if they had chosen him, so every night, before he turned the bedroom light off, he would smile in gratitude at the beauties on his wardrobe and say: "Goodnight ladies."

His dolls were in no way a compensation for the fact that he was forty and unmarried, as had been suggested to him more than once. That was a cheap shot spread about by certain people who should have known better. But such remarks never worried him; he had been able to carry on with the private joys of collecting by completely ignoring them.

Then everything changed from the moment that Maryelle Blomm had agreed to marry him — under what she termed "certain essential conditions". The first reform she demanded was that Morton get rid of the dolls from the bedroom. She said it was too spooky being spied on in bed by her glass-eyed competitors. Her second instruction was to pack up the dolls in the living room and store them in the garage. Maryelle pointed out that they hardly left any room for visitors. The third condition was financial. Morton had been a bachelor too long and didn't understand how modern couples shared joint bank accounts.

What a fool she made of him. For all his forty years of caution, Morton turned out to be as dumb as they come. In fact, thirty thousands dollars' worth of dumb. All of it in hard-earned savings. Maryelle simply went to the bank, cleaned out his account, then shot through. Morton had been suckered.

The night he discovered that Maryelle and his money had gone, Morton unpacked his dolls again. Then he started with a knife in the living room and worked his way through to the bedroom.

Like a serial killer, he methodically disembowelled the fairytale characters, hacked the limbs off the ballerinas, decapitated the fairy princesses and brutally butchered the brides. The carnage was horrific.

It took a good hour to do a complete job on them all. Then Morton went to bed. "Goodnight ladies," he said with a smile, before turning the light out.

Departure Time
Barry Southam

His attitude to tipping should have warned her, Angela would later tell her closest friend. It's those little messages that count. Ignore your gut response at your peril. Bryan had been a right prat in the restaurant not long after they first met, refusing to contribute to a tip with the rest, after some great service from a young student working his way through art school as a waiter at night. Reckoned tipping was just a yank guilt trip for letting employers pay lousy wages, and should not be imported into New Zealand. Then there was the incident with the Asian stall holder at the flea market. Bryan took great delight in beating him down for an original Jane Evans painting that was already a bargain, due to the man's ignorance of New Zealand painters. She had remonstrated that he did not have to be so harsh, the stallholder had to make a living and was already missing out significantly. Bryan refused to listen, snapped at her about living in the real world.

All these messages ignored, swamped by hormones or something. Bryan had a lovely smile, made her laugh, it was spring, and he had the loveliest flat in Parnell, so central, close to her work.

Moving in was a definite mistake. If Angela had started to wonder before about his money attitude, once she was sharing everything she discovered he was like Scrooge on speed, she told Miriam.

"He had this idea that we should sign a property agreement, so if we broke up he wouldn't have to ante up half of what he had. I told him that it only applied to married couples in New Zealand, not de facto ones, but he went and checked up anyway."

Power consumption was another recipe for a row. She did not turn the lights off after her, showered far too much and too long, left stove elements on after she cooked.

"He keeps telling me that he does not have shares in Power New Zealand, as if it would make any difference if he did."

Miriam sympathised, sipped her coffee, and left. Heard it all before. Angela returned home to find Bryan ready to do his volcano act again, this time over the toll bill. She tried to explain the importance of the Melbourne calls to her other best friend, recently divorced. Not a chance. She watched him vomiting words, thinking he reminded her of a deep sea fish her father used to catch. Their eyes also used to bulge, if they were hauled to the surface too fast. What were they again? Hapuka. That's right. Then a wrong remark from her and he turned from hapuka to shark. Attacked her, bruising her arms, ripping her blouse.

She rang her friend in Melbourne, who was delighted at the prospect of Angela coming to live with her, guaranteed she would get a better job, better pay.

Angela booked her tickets to coincide with Bryan going away on a two week business trip down south. She had made sure that the Telecom account was still in his name, and arranged to fly out the day after he had gone. The last thing she did as she left the flat was dial the 24-hour speaking clock in New York and leave the phone off the hook.

City, Coast, Man, Child
Tina Shaw

The Indian man comes down off the track and onto the beach with a child, a baby, in a backpack. The shingle beach echoes beneath his feet as if it is hollow beneath. He looks a little pale, perhaps sickly, although that could be the hike down from civilisation. He greets us, as we loll on the pebbles and lick our gaze over the sea, and continues on his way. It is easy to talk about hindsight. I have promised to travel to India, with a woman who wants to explore the continent by train. I have mentioned the fact that Indian trains tend to be overcrowded and often derail, but she is oblivious to everything but the adventure. This Indian man, on the shingly beach of Hekerua, must surely know about such trains, must surely know how privileged we all are, being able to sit on this isolated beach and yet be able to reach the city within forty minutes. The Sky Tower is a constant reminder of sophistication, and on the distant horizon, if you stand in the right spot, it dominates the CBD as if it were the key to a mythical city. Our black puppy runs down to the water and back again, afraid yet not afraid.

City, coast, man, child. The Indian man makes his way across the pebbled beach, and up onto the track on the other side.

Two days later we are walking along the cliff track. The weather has changed, and the sea is a restless piece of washing threatening to blow off the line at any moment; a tiny wooden launch has been dashed onto rocks and lies in pieces in a corner of Sandy Bay. The puppy is enthusiastic, off her lead, and is charging ahead, when the Indian man appears. The child (not a baby after all) is teetering forward on the path in front of the man's long legs, unconfined by the backpack.

The puppy bounds ahead, delighted by the child. The child tumbles, blown over by the dog, and falls past the wire fence and down the bank, landing head down against a manuka trunk. We scramble, horrified, to retrieve such a delicate object, terrified of damage. Yet it is all over in a moment.

The Indian man props the child back onto its feet. It is all right, he says, the child is fine. You are fine, he says, to the child. As if the child has not just survived a life-threatening plunge down a possible cliff face. He doesn't even shout at us, does not even weep for what might have happened.

We continue, but the weather has packed in. The child's face remains in my mind, wan and submissive, as if he had been fully expecting dogs to push him over banks for so long and was quite used to the idea. He really likes dogs, the Indian man kept saying, as if it was merely a chance dog encounter on the street. I want to shake him; I want to kiss his child.

That night I dream of a curly-haired baby boy. The next day I buy a gift for the man, a fern, and for the following days I take the fern with me on my walks. It may take days: we don't know where he lives, this Indian man, except that he walks the coastal path with his little child. The fern becomes like a walking companion: do you see that island? That is Rakino. Those are the Noises. Do you think it will rain? In the city I would feel self-conscious carrying everywhere with me a potted fern, no matter how attractive, wrapped up in a piece of yellow glazed paper and pale twisted ribbon. But not here. For here, I know, one day soon I will again meet an Indian man who carries a backpack, within which resides a child, unfairly treated, who has the face of a madonna.

Kelly Wuz Here
Rhonda Bartle

Today was a good day. Not like yesterday. Yesterday was a grey day. I only got five toots. Five toots, three waves and one guy who leaned a long way out his window and shouted, "Ooooh Baby!" Today was better. Seven toots, four wolf-whistles and a couple of blasts from a Kenworth. And some old bag who gave us the fingers, but we won't count her.

Everything round here is covered in graffiti: Wank. Screw. Fuck off. This is not outer suburbia, it's bloody urban scrawl.

"You should be thankful," my mum says, "for a subsidised place."

I should sit here day after day and watch the wallpaper skin off the walls? Wait for the drunk next door to start banging on the door? Turn the telly up full blast so I can't hear the bawling?

"Beggars can't be choosers," says my mother from her town house that's not big enough for three. "Visit when you can."

"Don't be stupid," I say, "I don't have a car. The buses don't run this far out. Where's the money for a taxi?"

"Ring whenever you want a chat."

"Righto," I say, "ET phonnnne hommme. What phone? I'll send smoke signals," I tell her. "Or you listen out for the sound of the drums."

"No need to be sarcastic," she sniffs. "It's not my fault," which really means, Whose fault is it, then? She's been dying to say it, only she's never got the guts. She's like a little kid who's learning how to ride a bike, going from point A to point B but with a lot of pissing about in between.

"Ring from the shops," she tells me. "How hard can that be?"

Not that hard. We start walking to the shops every day, Cherry and me. All men are perves. They leer out the windows and yell crazy things at me battling along with my kid in her pushchair. I chopped all my tights into shorts and my tops into Band-aids, so they'd really have something to look at. My legs are getting hard like those tarts from the gym. My shoes are falling to bits, but they'll do. If I come across an accident, maybe I'll sneak some off a body.

I say to Cherry, "It's a blue day," or a white day, or a yellow day, according to the weather. We start out around ten o'clock and then we're back for lunch, though I don't feel much like eating when I'm home. Cherry has a bottle, then we have a nap, down together like the spoons in the KFC packs that get blown around the place. And that's when we tally up.

Today was a good day. Yellow. Seven toots, four wolf-whistles and a couple of blasts from a Kenworth. And then there was that guy outside the phone box as we stood and only glared at it again.

"Wanna ride?" he asked.

"No thanks," I said, digging my name into Telecom's door with a tear tab. "We're walking."

The Mural
Graeme Lay

For Ms Hermione Hughes (42), M.Sc.(Hons) Dip. Ed., the schoolgirl mural was the stone end. It appeared on the wall of the Pleasure House as if by black magic. One morning the high front wall of the building was its usual plain pink, the next it was emblazoned with the huge mural. It must have been painted, with typical furtiveness, during the night.

The sight of it nearly caused Hermione to drive her Volkswagen into a power pole as she came up the rise to Central College for Girls, where she was headmistress. The youngest headmistress in the school's history. And now, the angriest. She felt her stomach tighten into a knot as she stared at the mural.

A girl, dressed in the green uniform of Central College. With certain modifications. She was portrayed from the back, bending right over, peering back through her wide apart legs. Her gym skirt so short that there was a strip of naked flesh between the tops of her long black stockings and the clips that held them to her suspender belt. Between her long legs was her face — an undeniably beautiful face — pouting provocatively. The girl had flaxen plaits, each tied in a red ribbon. And underneath the muralist had painted boldly in green and in a fair imitation of an adolescent hand, "COME IN AND PLAY".

Hermione was not a prude, she was always careful to point out in her letters to the newspapers protesting at the massage parlours' brazen advertising. She was unmarried, but she had a lovelife nonetheless, one that was an enigma only to those who had never tasted its delights. No, she was not a prude. What raised her ire about the mural was its shameless exploitation of young women. That, and its provocative nature. Who knew what the male monsters who lurked in the shadows of the city would do when inflamed by an image like that?

Hermione drove on to the college, withdrew into her office, made herself a strong cup of coffee. She knew who was responsible. Haydon Rasty, the beast who owned nearly all the parlours in the area, who had painted every one in murals of semi-clad women. Most with breasts bare, one with a lash, another with a gaping reddened mouth. She had protested to the authorities for years now, but even the Christian-riddled council seemed powerless to combat the grossly offensive signage.

Hermione put down her cup, glanced into her office mirror, brushed her hair, touched up her makeup. This time Rasty had gone too far. This time she would take him head on. In his lair.

She pressed the bell of the Pleasure House, trying not to glance up at the crotch of the mural girl, slyly designed to appear just above the door. Hermione pressed again. The door opened. A woman, about 50, chewing gum. Tight blue dress, heavy makeup, dead blonde hair. When she saw Hermione she lifted her chin disdainfully.

"Yes?"

"I want to see the manager."

The sluttish woman paused in her chewing. "He's busy."

Hermione steeled herself. "I don't care. *I need to talk to him.*"

The woman sighed, shook her head. "He won't see you, dear."

Dear. Hermione drew herself up to her full five feet two. "I want to see the manager, and I want to see him *now.*"

The woman stopped chewing, put her head on one side in an unmistakeable gesture of pity. Still studying the headmistress, she shook her head slowly.

"It's no good, dear. You're not nearly pretty enough to work here."

They Know How to Care
Jenny Jones

The doctor at the hospital introduced himself and explained the procedure. I would lie in that comfortable chair over there and he would look through his microscope (there) at my cervix (over there) and I would be able to watch on that screen (up there). Then we would have a little chat and discuss options. I could ask for more information at any time and there was no hurry about anything. I did not have to do anything I didn't want to and I should let them know if there was anything I wanted — a change perhaps.

"A change?" Did he mean a holiday?

"A change from me."

But I'd only just met him and he hadn't even put his white coat on.

He went away to let me undress with modesty. I was given a curtained-off corner of the room so I didn't even have to take my clothes off in front of the nurse. She asked how my day was going and if I would please call her by her Christian name. It took some ingenuity to introduce "Maureen" naturally and in the time allowed.

"My day's fine, thank you Maureen."

I wasn't nervous. I believed what they'd told me, my GP and the family planning clinic before that — that there was no cause for alarm. Even if it was cancer, they'd be able to cut it out and make me new again. The problem of the leaking water-pipe under my driveway had been left at home. I relaxed. It was like going to the dentist — knowing I was in expert hands.

Together the doctor and I examined my cervix. It was all go. Mucous was pouring out of ducts and swirling like gauze scarves across the screen. A little crevice, the same that had opened to admit my children to the world, shied secretively from the doctor's inquisitive cotton bud. Not far away, the abnormal cells, a honeycomb of lighter colour, lodged like the unwelcome guests they were, but I didn't mind, because I was in good hands — until Maureen put her arm around me.

Was there something they weren't telling me or did they expect me to swirl into irrational panic? Afterwards we sat, the doctor and I, and discussed my options. He suggested I come back for further treatment, when he would excise the offending parts with a wire loop. I remembered that as well as offering me a change, he had encouraged me to ask questions.

"It's not a biopsy?"

"I never said it was." He looked like a man who'd mislaid his breastplate.

The next day I rang up for additional information. Maureen couldn't remember who I was. "But Maureen," I wanted to say, "I'm *Fiona.*"

I'm sure I'm in good hands. It's just why can't they act normal? Like my dentist.

In My Father's House
Jane McKenzie

In my father's house we hang on the walls. It is not my mother's house but she is there, just out of sight in the laughing group of her children, reflected in a smile, recalled in a face.

We hang on the walls beside the children of my father's wife, on display to each other. How nice, people say, that you all get on so well, just one big happy family; how lucky you are to have two homes.

Silently, captured in a freeze-frame of years, we bear witness to a frenzy of christenings, Christmases and unguarded holidays. Our bad haircuts always with us along with the tinsel and threatening tantrums. Much is out of shot; only things that fit the frame should stay.

We call ourselves still-life with movement. A new baby, a growing cousin, a second husband signal a rearrangement of the gallery, a jostling for position; and surreptitiously, on each visit, we sniff around the familiar corners like suspicious dogs.

Have we been moved to the back? Who the hell is that? In the delicate hierarchy of family, we want to know our place. Checking, just checking, we tell ourselves, accepting another glass and feigning interest in a step-cousin's new house. (Our pictures are more intimate than we are. They at least would know each other if they found themselves relocated to the top of the stairs one night. They have history.)

Repackaging the past to prime the present has its hazards. Dredging up the sixties one night with a slideshow, giggling at our puny selves doing headstands in impossibly green paddocks, we are transfixed by the sudden appearance of a lone skier. Who is that masked man?

A frantic rearrangement of the slides ripples through the darkened room and we are uneasy. His white frostiness is a startling intrusion into our warmth; we are mesmerised because suddenly we know him. He is my father's wife's first husband, father to some of us, godfather to others. Dead, now. Suicide. But still behaving unexpectedly.

"How did that get in there?" Muttering, across the room.

How could it not be in there? we ask ourselves. Apparently, the dead can refuse to be edited.

My mother is not dead. She is just not present; although she, too, makes an appearance that evening, smiling hopefully out of an open window at Milford with her hair in a French roll.

The slideshow is over; much more reliable, we silently agree, than the other stills on the walls.

In my mother's house we hang on her words. They don't always match what we see in my father's house and for every picture my mother can summon a great deal more than a thousand words. They put flesh on our family bones.

On the drive home my husband reaches for my hand. My second husband, who thought families were toxic until he met mine.

"Well, that wasn't so bad, was it?"

I concentrate on the road and wonder, who will hang on our walls?

Vibrations
Catherine Mair

After reading her poem he wrote to her. He said, I feel rays of healing colours. They transcend space. The vibrations are right. He signed his letters with extravagant kisses. Big, sloppy, ragged ones.

She fluttered like a moth.

Being tuned to vibrations also, her best friend bought new curtains for her bedroom. The composer posted his poems to her and she typed them in a minor key.

She paid the postage to the editors. The editors failed to pick up the vibrations expected of them.

All else went well. He posted cassette tapes of his concerts. He told her of his admiration for Scriabin. She played arrangements for piano on Sunday afternoons.

He wrote that he would appear from long distance to find her. She trembled with something akin to shock or desire. She typed a cool, yet come-hither reply.

In the morning the electrical storm left a strange singing in the wires. When the wind dropped she had a sudden sensation of emptiness.

She forgave her composer's defection to Poland with a soprano as he continued to send her his love poems. The soprano, after all, was only a friend, though this glitch may have made her receptive. Then enter smash palace.

At the soiree she draped herself over the arm of the stock car driver's chair. He got the message. He coated his paws with flour to soften his vibrations. She considered the likely hands of the musician. She summed up the eyes and hands of the driver.

She considers, she is considering. She has had a bad winter but summer is coming. And her friend has bought her a tiny, expensive brooch from the Vatican.

Now is the Hour
Steve Whitehouse

"Haven't we met somewhere before? I'm Trevor Rowe."

I was going to say yes, then thought better of it.

The enquirer was my age, early 50s and greying. I am bald, distressingly thick around the waist and have recently taken to wearing glasses. So it wasn't surprising he wasn't sure. We'd only met once, thirty years before, on the other side of the world. I didn't think he would even recall my name.

I was looking at an old photo the other day. It was taken in Trafalgar Square and I was impressively skinny: handlebar moustache, shoulder length hair, bell bottom trousers. Carnaby Street style.

Jenny was in the picture too. Strange to think that mini skirts have come back into fashion. She certainly had the legs for them. Probably still has. She'd come to Europe on a working holiday. Trevor was her old boyfriend from Auckland and had turned up in London to join her just days before. I'd always rather fancied her at University so I'd agreed to drive them down to Dover where they were leaving by ferry on a hitch-hiking tour around France and Italy.

I went on board to see them off. When Trevor went off to buy some sandwiches, Jenny burst into tears.

"I don't know why I'm doing this," she sobbed. "Trevor talked me into this trip and I didn't have the heart to say no. I really don't like him any more. Not like that, anyway. I just can't bear the thought of three months"

"Look," I said, thinking quickly. "You get off the boat and wait for me. I'll keep him busy."

She hurried off and Trevor reappeared. "She's in the lavatory," I explained. A loudspeaker called for visitors to disembark. "Have a good trip," I mumbled.

When the ferry pulled out, there was Trevor on the deck, Jenny and I on the dock. She mimed a lot in "I'm really sorry" body language.

"Don't you get any ideas," she said to me, dabbing at her mascara as we got into my Mini. We drove back to London and that was about it. My main memories of the next two years are of cold water flats, shilling-in-the-slot gas meters and dreary temp jobs. I know one was supposed to enjoy the great OE, but that wasn't my experience. I missed the blue blue skies and the green green leaves. I wonder what the me of then would make of the me now. And vice versa. Would we like each other, or would we disapprove?

"Met before?" I replied. "No, I don't think so."

Some things are best left unremembered.

Sea Change
Julia Oakley

It was a perfect day to be out on the water, and for once he could appreciate the appeal of the city that was otherwise just a soulless landmark to 1980s greed. While there was no denying it took money to gain access to the Hauraki Gulf in anything more luxurious than a dinghy, the sea itself didn't care who you were. Didn't give a stuff about inflated egos and exaggerated self-importance.

Nevertheless his chest swelled with satisfaction as he piloted the boat out of the marina and into the harbour, nodding to the skipper of a yacht to starboard. His lungs drank in the cool salt air. Yep, this is the good life, he mused. This is what it was all about, after all those years of working his guts out. Now was the time to reap the rewards.

His gaze rested on Miranda, soaking up the sun on the foredeck, her coltish blonde hair tousled by the breeze, her juicy young breasts squeezed into a tiny, blue daisy bikini top. Content just to sunbake behind her Raybans she took it all for granted, as if it were simply her due. He knew if it weren't his boat she was stretched out on it would be someone else's. Some other old fool's.

His ex-wife's words seemed to float above him at the strangest times, accusing him, like the yellow eyes of the seagull that hovered over the boat like a mascot.

"Hello, Trudy," he greeted it fondly. "So the divorce isn't final yet."

After all this time, he still felt a twinge of guilt whenever he took a bimbo out on the boat. Despite their domestic squabbles on land, he'd always felt close to his wife on the water and, even now, she still seemed to hold him in her spell. It was worse at night. He'd awaken an hour or so after having reminded the girl of the moment that she loved more about him than his money, only to find himself restless, lonesome and unable to sleep. He'd feel an irresistible pull to go up on deck and just sit there, watching the moon on the black water, listening to the wash lapping the boat, the wind creaking like an unquiet ghost.

Sometimes he thought he could see Trudy in the water, sleeping like Shakespeare's Ophelia, her long hair floating like seaweed.

And although he knew she was, in fact, very much alive and happily remarried to a better man than he, he still felt responsible for the slow and painful death of something inside her. Her carefree nature? Her youth? Maybe that was what he was doing – trying to recapture the innocence, the hope of those early years. Exiled from his wife's companionship, he felt destined to spend the rest of his life playing some increasingly seedy character in endless reruns of a nautical soft-porn movie, trying to convince himself, the bimbos, Trudy and the world that he'd got it made.

The bird knew different.

A Foot in the Door
Bernard Brown

That time will always be with me.

Earlier in the day I had mailed to London my manuscript on the application of Vaihinga's *Philosophy of As If* to fictions in physics and law. A mouthful. A half-million words' mouthful. Impressive stuff. Never had I felt so good about life or been so much in love.

Ernestine's family was visiting from Adelaide. It would be our first meeting and my chance to do the splendid old-fashioned thing and beg the parental permission to marry her. Ernestine and I had met only weeks before, but there was no doubt in our minds.

Dressed precisely, as she had advised (they were "of the manse", Ernestine said, and "dear old conservative plonks"), I contrived to be five minutes late at the hotel and a tiny bit breathless. I apologised – the book had delayed me. They straightaway warmed, as she had assured me they would. ("Maddy and Fee" – the twin sisters – "will be giggly but Pa will play the silly old vicar and set you at ease. And Mummy will balance a tear on her cheek.")

Exactly as Ernestine had predicted. As in the family photo I had seen, all had a little bit of Ernestine about them. Except, that is, for her touch of artless coquetry.

Temptress! Pussycat!

Not a natural small-talker, nevertheless the right words came to me – about their flight over and their first thoughts about the city. It was rehearsed, but I could tell from Ernestine's eyes that it was OK.

A twin (Fee?) awkwardly approached and put a glass of something sparkling in my hand. I made a little pun. Quiet, appreciative laughter. But this prettyish, chubby lass (fourteen or so) seemed to wince. Momentarily, but distinctly. A sniffy creature? Perhaps she resented my sudden incursion into their lives. As a younger sister might.

She and her non-identical sibling clasped hands and, as if prearranged, went off to another room of the suite.

Ernestine, across the lounge, began to reiterate how we had met; to pave the way for my essential speech ("popping the question", as she had put it over the phone). Her mother — neat, greying, handsome — moved toward me with a plate of vol-au-vents. As I took one she stiffened, much as the awkward Fee had, and darted the oddest look at me, then over to her husband.

All this, for whatever cause, was beginning to be difficult. There was a *longueur*. I cast about for something to fill it and walked as I spoke to the quite decent Modigliani print close by Father and Ernestine. Good. It would get me to E. and the comfort of her hand.

Father twitched, winced. Was this some kind of family foible? And he paled, stopping my sentence in its tracks. A glance (again) — this time from husband to wife. Chins tilted.

Ernestine had cupped her palm in mine. Thank God. Then the unthinkable. Hers went cold. Dead cold. As frozen as the last lines of the Vaihinga text I had just sent off. She let go.

I tried to say something about the sureness of swift dalliance. And, nightmarishly, I heard my every word. The three of them stood stock-still. Askance. Silent and looking straight through me.

There was a stifled, dreadful giggle from the other room.

I knew I had to leave. The blanched, totally bleak face of Ernestine was plain about that. Mumbling something, I turned and found the door — mercifully ajar. Behind me, my name was chokingly half said, half called to the mother's consolatory "Nownow" Finito. Kaput.

But why? I asked myself as I stumbled from the hotel. It was as if, almost as if I had said the f word, or deliberately left my fly open. And, of course, I hadn't. It was as if I had stood in something. As of course, I had.

Knife Dance
Prue Toft

I fell in love with Bessie Norris when she fell off the kitchen table and a knife shot up her nose. She was dancing to a popular tune at the time, but that is not the whole truth, because I was not there. Bessie recounted the story to me in a Ponsonby bar. Her story made my vitals contract into a fist that was at once both horror and desire.

In the silence that fell between us, the seconds marked off by a thudding background bass, I felt obliged to supply an injury in return. All I had done was enquire about the arrow-shaped mark on her nose. Too late, I realised, my tale of a scar caused by zipped-up flesh was both paltry and ignominious. A shamefully crimped pucker up my belly could not compare with her brand of exuberance.

I saw her in my mind's eye, high kicking on the table, thick gold ropes of hair flying to the ceiling. Who could call such magnificence "pig tails". No, these braids were so heavy and silken they could have drawn back opera curtains.

She was huge, golden, and seamless, apart from the scar on her left nostril. She was wrapped in a fabric of large scarlet peonies. Her breasts filled it like the arm rests of a Sanderson linen sofa. Her skin colour ripened from the clotted cream of her throat to golden queen on her cheeks. Her teeth were white, large and perfectly square. Monet, Rubens, Degas.

I bought her another green ginger wine. My eyes were drawn to her smooth ankles with the faintest gloss on the shins, jiggling in time to the music. A black drawstring crochet purse dangled from one wrist.

I dismounted from my bar stool to find the loo. I needed time to think. My head reeled with plans to impress. I breathed her name in steam on the mirror and drew the time out fiddling with my hair and dusting fluff off my jacket. I planned a table for her. Waxen headed tulips drooping over platters of smoked salmon. A slashed crown rib oozing pink meat juices beaded with oil. Crystal wine glasses with strings of straw-coloured bubbles bursting on the surface.

Turning carnivore, I pictured the indented crescent my teeth would leave on her downy shoulder. The one exposed when her dress slipped to one side. Not hard enough to leave a plummy bruise, but firm enough for a neat, dental cast.

As the loo door swung shut behind me I saw him saunter towards her. There was music in the roll of his pelvis. Chrome bullet burnished studs flashed on his jacket. Steel danced in the glint in his eye. A cigarette hung from his bee-stung lips. Creaking leather boots, a spotted bandanna. Jessie James, Billy the Kid, Ned Kelly.

The bar stool was empty by the time I reached it, save the vibrating air from her swinging lace purse and the blade flash of his backward glance.

London
Chris Harrison

It was hot and we were moving in time, perfectly synchronised. It seemed as if the whole universe was rocking with us. My chin pressing against the girl's forehead. Sweat running mostly from my brow down my nose. It hit my top lip and was then deviated by a quick swipe of my tongue onto my ski slope chin. It waterfalled onto her centre parting and down her forehead to her eyebrows where it seemed to dissipate. I don't know why. I couldn't see any of this, but I could feel it. I was young and relatively inexperienced in the company of women, but when you are this close there is no need to speak. So we didn't even try.

Her full breasts pushed into my wet, still T-shirted chest. Her nipples were flaccid and tired, and I must have been too, because my eyes were closed. It was an afternoon like no other I had experienced before. It was a hell of a summer's tube ride. I was lucky to make it to Clapham.

Smoke Screen
Michael Easther

He sauntered across the school playground in an effort not to draw attention to himself. When he reached the main gates, he looked left, looked right. No one was watching him. He scurried through the gateway and along the fence line until he reached a small clump of trees where he could safely hide. Crouching down, he reached for his cigarettes and quickly lit one.

With the first puff he felt more relaxed, though he was still fearful of being seen. The school rules about smoking were so very strict. He had already been caught once and given a warning. If they caught him again, he was for the high jump. Out.

He finished his cigarette. Now came the tricky bit, getting back into the school grounds. He sidled towards the gateway, peered carefully through. No one was looking in his direction. He slid through into the playground, nonchalantly strolled towards the school entrance. Just then the bell for the end of recess sounded. Perfect timing. All he needed to do was wander along to the schoolroom, sit down behind his desk and start teaching his next class of boys.

The Pond
Peter Bland

A childhood love of water was the beginning of his troubles. Streams to start with. And oceans were good. But his greatest love was for the small pond hidden in thick wooded fields near his home. This was where he fished and skimmed stones but, mostly, he just lay in the grass admiring the bronzed dragonflies that flickered between the reeds. The pond was where he went to be alone. It was better than home. Home was for people you hardly knew and visitors who never arrived. Once, before he was born, his parents must have been young and happy and travelled to distant lands. Now, they were old and tired and stranded among the memories of some former life. The house was full of chairs made of elephants' feet; vases full of hippopotamuses' teeth; dried snakeskins nailed to the stairs. But, best of all was the old leather suitcase left in the hall, as though – at any moment – someone might still find the energy to leave. It was covered in labels from Aden to Zanzibar.

After his parents died, when he was still only fourteen, he was left the old suitcase along with his father's best pair of shoes and 30 pounds from the sale of the hippopotamuses' teeth. With this small inheritance he headed happily into the unknown. But the pond went with him. When he rented a basement room off the Edgware Road, the pond was still there, in the suitcase, under his father's shoes. He couldn't remember packing it, although he had visited the pond to say goodbye on his way to the station. It must have sneaked inside the case when he wasn't looking. He tried to pour it down the sink, but the basin got blocked up with dead leaves. He tried to give it away, but no one wanted something as personal as a pond. He grew restless and tried to shake it off by visiting a number of foreign countries, but – at the last moment — he could never bring himself to leave the damp suitcase behind.

When he finally settled down on a beautiful island in the South Pacific, he tried to dry the pond up by leaving the suitcase open in the sun. The leather cracked and the pond turned to mud, but the green silty water always bubbled back at night.

He grew fond of his Pacific island, in spite of the odd cannibal and the tourists. He learned the language and married the daughter of a chief. He was accepted by his new neighbours as a true tribal brother, until they spotted the pond. The suitcase was bad enough, with its British Empire labels and its dated Edwardian leather, but the pond was beyond their understanding.

"We don't have ponds here," they told him, "anymore than we have becks, or rills, or babbling brooks, or any other of that dated old-world rubbish. You should have left the pond where it belongs!"

"I tried," he explained, "but it's part of my childhood."

"Then you should put away childish things," they said, as they danced and sang their tribal songs.

Once the pond was seen as a threat by his new friends they turned their backs on him. Even his wife went back to her mother. It was then that the pond began taking up more and more of his time. It seeped into all his thinking. In spite of the mosquitoes, he would stare at it for hours, just as he had as a child. One day, overcome with curiosity, he stepped inside. Down and down he sank into endless muddy depths. A feeling of overwhelming peace swept through him as he let go of everything, his name, his shape, his history. And then he was gone. The last thing he remembered was the scent of the pond, faint, forgiving, far back.

Testrip 100 Bucks
Virginia Were

It's ten to six and the gallery is full. I meant to get there earlier only the bus went past the stop and I had to run up the hill. I do a quick sweep of the walls, catalogue in hand, and *Paid* jumps out. It's a work by Billy Apple that says "Artists have to live like everybody else." I have a headache from trying to make up my mind.

OK, I've made my choice and I'm second in the queue, nervously looking at my watch. A man pushes in front and is told to get in the queue. He wants Billy's work as well. At 5.55 we're allowed to start. The guy in front of me buys *Paid* and money changes hands, receipts are given out. I'm second in line and I buy John Reynolds' work *Swan Song for K-Rd*. A wonky red watercolour star which reminds me of a Christmas card. There's some image in the background behind the red star but I can't tell what it is. The man behind me buys a work by Ronnie van Hout called *I Love Me, I Love Me Not*. We sit next to each other on the vinyl sofa writing cheques. Ronnie's work is made of brightly coloured felt and reminds me of sewing classes at school, also a felt bookmark with a cat's face on it I once found in a library book. Someone is busy with the red stickers. They spread like a virus across the walls. The works are going fast. I wonder if I missed anything and decide I should have bought Peter Roche's fluorescent tube with the plastic fruit, but I didn't see it behind the door. Now it's too late. Julian buys Ani O'Neill's work, *Tangaroa*, a stuffed doll with a huge penis. He says it's for Leo to play with.

Billy is wearing his yellow glasses. He tells me about a sound work he is doing off Big Sur in California. The work will be underwater. I imagine him in a wetsuit tumbling backwards over the side of a boat. Instead of the yellow glasses he wears a diving mask. He has only just learned to dive. "It's amazing the things I do for art," he thinks to himself as he descends through bands of colour. He plans to make another work on Pitt Island in the Southern Ocean. "I'm going there next month," he says. "This will be the first work of the millennium." I notice he always wears his shirts buttoned up to the collar. I want to ask for more detail but decide against it. He smiles when I tell him the first three people in the queue wanted his work.

Tessa Laird has made a work called *Chunky Pundit*. Hindu cards pinned to the walls. "But how would you hang it?" asks Brett. Dick Frizzell's paint splotch *Cosmic Yolk* has a red sticker next to it, and Billy tells Brett to buy Denise Kum's *Blot*. I drink a beer too quickly and stand in front of *Swan Song for K-Rd*. Perhaps there's a reference to K-Rd in there somewhere? I notice the fuchsia woman from Julian's opening is there. This time the fuchsia jacket is under her arm. I check to see if her nails are blue, but they're not. I wonder if she's bought anything?

Walking down Queen Street to catch the ferry we notice someone has stolen a panel from the mural outside the Town Hall. A sign pasted to the mural says, "Could whoever stole Nigel Brown's panel please return it."

Ghost Story
Elspeth Sandys

It had been a shitty day. My two are sixteen and twelve. The elder, a girl, is a typical teenager, alternately sullen and delightful. The younger, a boy, is pubescent, and will probably drive me to an early grave. Their father is not in this story. He ran off a year ago with a woman younger and richer (though not thinner; at least I have that) than me. She — her name's Pandora — has three children under seven so my two have become superfluous. Those of you who are solo parents will understand.

A shitty day, the third of our holiday. Rain, thickened with mist and wind. A walk in the woods which left us all looking like sewer rats. Back to our rented cottage only to find the water hadn't reheated since the morning. Bad temper all round till I hit on my idea.

"How would you like to go up on the moor? You could practise your driving (this to my daughter) on that old airfield."

The suggestion, once I'd promised my son he could have a turn too, was received rapturously.

The light was falling as I turned the car in through the ruined gates. We couldn't see much (this Cornish rain, unlike our rain at home, obscures the material world), but the slope of the hangar roofs caught whatever light there was. These days the hangars are used to store hay. Sheep wander in an out of the old accommodation block.

I stopped the car, and let my daughter take the wheel. She's going to make a good driver. Back home she'd have her licence by now, but in this country she has to wait till she's seventeen.

She'd just started to pick up speed when I yelled at her to stop.

"Look!" I ordered.

"Jesus, Mum".

"The hangar. Look. It's all lit up."

"Probably the farmer."

"Look!" I urged again.

She turned the engine off. My son put his hand on my shoulder. There were lights everywhere now, in the living quarters, in the mess, beaming from a tower I'd never noticed before. First the buildings, then the runway, then the planes, beached like huge black sea birds, came into focus. It was like watching the slow exposure of a negative.

"Listen!" I whispered.

Band music was playing from the mess. I recognised it at once. "Glen Miller," I pronounced.

My eyes were working so hard they felt as if they might jump out of my face. I was looking for the airmen. Sons from America (I knew my history), destined to die in bombing raids over Germany. But not a soul stirred. The only creatures moving were sheep.

I screwed my eyes up tight. How could sheep be grazing so contentedly in such surroundings?

"You OK, Mum?" my son asked.

I looked again. Everything was as it should have been.

"Can we get on with it now?" my daughter whined.

Framed
Trish Gribben

The frame he bought for the photograph was more ornate than he really wanted; the swirls and crests of Mexican silver were a distraction, reminding him of too many journeys with too many other women.

When he first saw the photograph he was taken aback. The blood pumped from his guts to his brain, hitting him with a force he didn't understand, barb-wire knots tightening between his shoulder blades. It was years since he had felt such a surge. He thought he had managed to dispel it, that devilish dance inside him whenever she came near his orbit.

But now there she was, framed. Forever, as long as he chose, in front of him on his black executive desk. Walking away. Dancing into the big blue. Free as a gull. (*Dammit, when have I ever felt like that?*)

The sand she trod on was a toffee gold. Nothing but her footsteps ruffled the surface left by the outgoing tide, no seaweed, no driftwood, no frills whipped up by a wind. The sea was calm and blue, rippled, with just one lacy little wave running up towards her toes. The sky was bright blue overhead, fading down to a wisp of grey clouds on the horizon.

Her nakedness was almost complete. Only the beloved silver bangle from Kathmandu clung to her wrist as she raised her arms towards the sky in a dance of celebration. Her body looked perfect, unfettered, unaltered, poised lightly on the elegant trim legs. (*Those bloody legs, how she loved to flaunt them.*) The boyish hips curved out slightly from her waist; there was no sag to her bum, only a slight telltale flattening.

Suddenly he picked up the frame for a closer look. My God, yes, there were a few wrinkles where the skin circled round her shoulder blades, a few more around her waist. (*The bitch, there has to be something.*) He looked harder. Of course, the hair was perfect, curls in a row, nothing straggling round her neck. A small flicker of amusement softened his lips. (*I bet the sea won't be allowed near that.*)

He could picture the next few moves: Quick strides into the cold wet. One, two, three, duck under, just as far as the chin. Half a dozen breast strokes along the beach, then back again. Head up to keep the hair dry, smile wide with delight. No matter that it was late autumn and the sunshine gave little warmth. When she saw the sea on such a day, in such a place, the clothes would be quickly shed and she would dance down to embrace it.

If he had been there to take the photograph, of course, it would never have happened. It was years, a lifetime, since she behaved like that with him. A fragment of memory shifted somewhere deep inside. He put the frame down and opened a drawer. His desk was no place for intimacy. Just for a moment he let tears flow.

It was unlikely he would ever get the chance. After all, a mother who would be ninety next month couldn't have that many swims ahead (*could she?*).

Over and Done
Kaye Vaughan

"I'll start digging first, if you like." Andrea grabs the spade and attacks the topsoil. This is the easy bit of a thoroughly nasty job and means she doesn't have to look at the sack on the ground beside them. The spiky grass and earth yields easily to her effort, but, man-fashion, Mike wants to take over. Let him then, Andrea thinks petulantly. If it hadn't been for her insisting, nothing would have been done and that that thing would still be there in the morning for her to face alone. It's just bloody typical – the whining tape winds round and round in her head – she goes away for one weekend and always, always has to face the music one way or another when she gets back. Ha! He's struck the layer of clay. Well, let him sweat.

Grunting, Mike throws his whole body into the job, using his manpower to break up the resistant dirt. Andrea turns away. Such a beautiful time of the evening, dusk turning to night. She wanders over to the tree and tests the grapefruit, taking only the discs that almost fall into her hand. Cradling the armload, she moves back to Mike. "Shall I do a bit more?" she asks. "Here, you hold these." He just glances at her and snorts. "It needs to be deeper than that," she says, "and longer. It'll never fit." Her horror of the dog digging it up. Oh God.

"That should do it." Mike turns, drags the sack to the hole and pushes it in, using the metal blade of the spade to arrange the shape. Andrea winces, thinking, "It's not enough, not nearly enough," though she knows it would be pointless to argue. He shovels some soil into the drop then raises the spade and brings it down, backwards, and whacks once, twice, three times. Mike shovels and whacks twice more, before finally standing back.

"There," he grins, "over and done."

Andrea watches him walk back to the house. It had been such a great weekend and she had looked forward to getting home. Slowing to turn into her driveway she saw the body. A horrified jogger swivelled to take a closer look before running on. Not his problem. But, Andrea realised grimly, it was hers. Obviously. Her first words on entering the house had been, "Did you know there's a dead cat at the top of the drive?" Of course he did. Then why the hell hadn't he done something about it? Her dog had greeted her ecstatically, sniffing and licking and she had shuddered to think of what he might do to the creature. If something wasn't done. If she didn't do something. Well, she had and now it was, as Mike had said, over and done.

Andrea pauses beside the unmarked grave; then, using her jumper as a crib for the grapefruit, she follows Mike into the house.

Waiting for the Tiger
Rachel Bush

"*On the day of the tiger hunt, this is the tiger hunt in India,*" she said, "I sat with the other women, the wives mainly, in a clump of trees for almost two-and-a-half hours. They gave me two cushions, one of black velvet and the other a nondescript satin one, so that I should not be uncomfortable sitting there so long in a tree. I forget its name now. An Indian kind of tree, where I could sit at the junction of two branches, shaded by its large leaves.

"I have never been so bored. We were not to speak. We were not to move. To divert myself, I inhaled deeply and tried to hold my breath, counting one hackety pack, two hackety pack, for sixty seconds. I was wearing a cream linen skirt which I had bought in Venice, and I smoothed the folds and looked at the details of the slub in it, anything to make the time pass.

"Also I tried to think about how my mother and my grandmother had to hide for two hours in a swamp, a raupo swamp, during the Maori Wars. She was only two at the time. They would have been killed if they hadn't left the house, and my grandmother was terrified my mother would cry and they would be discovered. So if they could do that, surely I must be able to wait in stillness for a tiger, which is supposed to be a pleasure.

"Mrs Beconsfield, the commissioner's wife, she's long dead now, I could see her clearly, how she slept across from me in her branch, quite upright and quite still, but her mouth had fallen open, a small dark cavity. Orifice, I thought of that word. Yet rather an alarming woman when she was awake.

"I was bored, I think I said that before, but the tiger did come. After two hours and twenty minutes we saw it. Such a beautiful animal, but savage of course, we knew that, and ready to kill. The men were lining it up in their sights – well, I think that is what it is called when they are directing their guns towards a target, getting ready to shoot.

"The discomfort was intolerable. I shifted slightly, and the cushion – the one with buff coloured satin covering it – fell from the tree. There had been such silence before, that it was itself like a gunshot or a thunderbolt. And, of course, the tiger was gone in great bounds in no time, and the men were angry, and their wives even angrier, and I never went to another tiger shooting the whole time I was in India."

Blueboy Explores the Hotspots
David Lyndon Brown

I must have been awaiting the events of that evening for a long time, because before I experienced them I dreamed them — the final *imprimatur* of reality.

"Just promise me," I said to Danny, "that Room 346 will contain nothing but memories." The armour of the soldiers fighting in the street chimed and glinted in the moonlight.

We had to take a shower before we were permitted to enter the building. I followed Danny under the cascade. Without his skin Danny looked like a different person. Pins of light danced off his body.

Danny took my hand and led me into the labyrinth. "Don't worry," he said. There were sensors embedded in the floor which registered the heat of our footsteps activating bolts of halogen lightning. The only sound was an amplified licking tongue.

As we reached the upper levels, Danny became more and more excited. I had difficulty keeping up with him. I suspected we were nearing Room 346. We passed a colonnade containing dozens of rooms where people were engaged in the mechanics of sex. They were barely visible behind a wall of blue silence. Danny was wearing a white shirt and blue trousers.

The Vista Lounge was full of foreigners. No two people spoke the same language. They had to communicate by means of loud signals. Danny became aroused by the cacophony. He pressed me towards the bar. It was dominated by a towering transvestite in a stiletto headdress. Danny passed me a drink. His eyes changed from blue to green. The drink contained shards of broken ice.

"Look," Danny said. I turned to see the cenotaph topple. Through the panoramic window the horizon was illuminated by explosions and detonations.

On the causeway Danny gently touched my face. I could hear the faint echo of his bones through his fingertips. His skin smelled of cordite. I realised then that there was a chance he could be a mercenary. I looked down to discover that my clothes had dissolved. There was a red glow burning inside my chest. Danny placed his lips between my nipples and a shaft of liquid passed between our bodies.

There were three enormous thuds like seismic sobs, rattling the chandeliers. Danny dragged me panting through the atrium in a hail of light. The air was dense with a green perfume called *Amaryllis Nervosa*.

In the piazza there was a market specialising in oriental pharmaceuticals. Danny led me to an enclosure where a veiled woman painted me from head to toe with a frond dipped in jasmine oil. Danny explained that it was an antidote to faithlessness and acrimony. We wept into a chalice and drank each other's tears.

Despite the music in the interminable corridors, the sweetest, most poignant music I have ever heard, I could not escape the perception that my footsteps were leading towards certain disaster. Danny stopped and produced a silver key from his pocket. He placed it in my hand. There was no number on the door.

Coffee-Frappé-Coco
Rachel Buchanan

Everyone always wears lipstick on Monday nights. Mine is Sahara Coffee, it's frosted brown. Lisa's is Coco Chic, peach in the gold tube, and Eva's is Raspberry Frappé, it's a cheap Barbie-doll brand but you know her. Tight as a bat's bum.

After we've put it on and had a pout, we always ask a couple of serious questions to get ourselves in the mood. "What would dolphins think?" I ask that and turn side-on to the mirror to see if my stomach is poking out. And "Is Freddie Mercury really dead?" That's Eva, she never got over the eighties when she ruled the dance floor at Lasers in that red tube skirt and studded double-belt. And Lisa normally asks, "Do you reckon Jackie Chan could karate kick under the ocean?" She likes to remind us that she met action Jack once when he was making a movie here. She said she was a black belt in relationships. He said, "Sorry? Speak up. Sorry?"

Then we wrap towels around our waists and go and sit on the seats and wait for him to arrive. The waiting is the best part. We all look at the clock and say to each other, he's late again and I bet he works three jobs and he probably cycles in from the Dandenongs or something. We enjoy imagining this very long ride. I mean, he's a very strong guy. He's huge.

He, our water aerobics instructor, usually comes about ten minutes late. We don't mind. He runs past the reception desk, pushing his racing bike with one hand, and bursts through the swing doors into the ladies' pool room like he's running through a footie banner. The doors go flap-flap-flap. We sprint in behind him, giving each other meaningful looks. I do a Staple into the *aqua profunda* — that's Italian for water that is profoundly deep. Lisa does a Freddie Flintstone —

that's when you sort of run really fast across the top of the water — and Eva does a Bomb. She's blonde.

We flash each other what's left of the Coffee-Frappé-Coco and watch Mr Big setting up the tape-deck. One night he played Dead Kennedys and we all went crazy doing the washing machine and the pogo stick. Other times he plays "We Are The Champions" by Queen ("punch the air, pump it, pump it") or "New York" by Frank Sinatra ("and stretch and release") or a hip-hop one that goes, *Truth is out of style I said truth is ...*

I really like it when he plays the truth song. It's for the profoundly deep segment when we use dumbbells to stay afloat and we kick our legs out to the left and stretch our arms out to the right and then reverse the process and everyone's swallowed at least a cup of chlorine. He asks us how we're feeling and we scream. Great. As the lipstick attests, we like to be in style.

Bones
Mabel Barry

When Tavita's sister rang to tell him that their aged mother had died in Apia, he went straight to the airport and booked a flight home.

It was evening when he arrived at Faleolo Airport, and his older sister and her children were waiting eagerly for him as he went through Customs. The drive to his Ma's home in Malifa was cool and pleasant. His sister explained to him that their mother had died suddenly and that the family had left all the arrangements for her funeral for him to carry out.

When they arrived they found the grandchildren preparing the food for the people who had come to pay their respects with gifts of fine mats and money.

Their old mother was dressed in white lace and was lying on the finest woven mats in the coolest corner of the house. She was surrounded by colourful ginger blossoms and sweet scented gardenias from her garden. As Tavita knelt by her, he saw that she had a happy smile on her face, and he thought that she looked lovely – for a ninety year old who had been a hard worker all her life bringing up a big family.

Tavita's father had died years earlier and was buried in the garden in front of the house. Their mother had wanted to be buried there next to him.

After their devotions and evening meal, Tavita and his sisters slept on the floor next to their mother's body. He told funny jokes to her and some of the women of the village came and sang songs all through the night. The grandchildren all slept in the bedrooms.

Early the next morning Tavita got up and began digging into his father's grave, searching for his father's remains. After he found his father's skull and bones, he laid them on an old mat and carried them into the house to be cleaned. The grandchildren watched him with awe as he sat cleaning and polishing the bones with great care.

"Don't be scared," he assured them, "this is what they used to do in the olden days. He held up his father's skull to show them how clean it was and they all ran away, frightened. "It's only your Grandpa," he called.

After he had completed his task, he wrapped his father's remains in a tapa cloth and left the bundle on his mother's old bed while he went to buy a coffin.

When he came back with his purchase, he carefully lifted his mother's frail body into the polished coffin lined with white satin. Then he went to fetch his father's remains.

But the bundle wrapped in the tapa was not where he had left it earlier. He went from room to room shouting, "Where is Grandpa?" The grandchildren who were decorating the coffin with all their little treasures, looked at him, wondering if he had lost his mind.

I want everyone in Grandma's bedroom," he ordered.

As they all trooped in, Tavita asked them in turn if anyone had touched the bundle wrapped in the tapa cloth. He was relieved when his oldest nephew brought the bundle out from under the big bed.

Tavita carried his father's remains and placed them in the coffin, at his mother's side. "Here is your husband," he told her.

The grandchildren all cried and clung to each other as the minister conducted the funeral service and the coffin was lowered. Tavita sang the Samoan farewell hymn with the others, happy that his mother and father were together again at last. Then, as the head of the family, he made the rule that no one else would be buried in front of the house.

The Life Class
Judy Parker

The male model, Raoul, struck a pose on the chaise longue. Five women took up their pencils and charcoal and began to sketch

Raoul, taken unawares by the slippery silk cushions, felt the stirrings of an untimely erection. Blushed to the tips of his toes. Wondered what on earth they would think.

Maggie of the tattooed forearms, who had a fetish for bottoms — the rounder and wrinklier the better — was engrossed in his posterior.

Teresa, who was late and very shortsighted, and who had broken her glasses falling up stairs, confined herself to the nearest toes.

Simone, who'd been out all weekend at a party, and who saw the world swim and pitch in triplicate, thought she was doing a still life.

Julia, who hadn't scored for some time and who'd been up three nights in a row watching blue movies, was beginning to wilt.

And Catherine, seventy-six and single, preoccupied by a growth on her own left breast, wondered if it was malignant and, if so, how long they'd given him.

"One minute to go," said the model.

Four women put down their pencils and charcoal. Yawned and stretched. The fifth was snoring softly.

"How about a more dynamic pose this time?"

The Bird Lady
Sally Fodie

It was a macabre scene. Botulism. Sick ducks with long limp necks. Unsupported heads rolling on the concrete. A portly woman with long greasy hair lifted each head in turn and gently prised open the bill, squirting medicine from a giant syringe. The sadness of inevitable loss hung in the air. It stirred a memory.

I was ten years old and wanted to be a vet. The cat was a stray, mangy and obviously suffering. I held the animal up so that all four limbs hung limply under its body. I had made my diagnosis and went about busily splinting and bandaging each limb. The cat died, and a while later I lost my aspiration to be a healer of animals.

The bird lady was talking, more to the ducks than to me. "The house has to be sold, you see. I only get half." From the side door of the garage a bald parrot squawked incessantly. More sick ducks lined the porch. "Well? Where's the bird? You brought one, didn't you? The medicine costs, you know, it doesn't come cheap."

I reached for my cheque book.

I had found the hawk floating in the harbour and got to it just before the swooping shags. I was afraid of its beak, but it was its claw that did the damage, tearing holes in my buoyancy aid. Proud eagle eyes watched from the bottom of my kayak. The drenched body too sick and weak to escape.

I had learned from the cat episode to seek expert help.

The bird lady followed me to the carton and watched as I lifted out the fallen harrier. The end came quickly for the hawk, as quick as the swing of an iron poker.

"You murdering bastard!" she spat. "You've been eating my ducks!"

The Prisoner
Judith White

The young woman, locked in the attic, looks from the small window above her desk onto the garden below.

Each day at lunchtime he comes, carrying his book in a plastic bag, to sit on the same park bench to read. He wears a white crisp shirt, and jeans. He is pale and beautiful with long black hair and a ring in his eyebrow, like the small beginnings of a silver thought bubble.

Today he has a large hardback. He sits with his back straight, and his legs crossed, turning the pages in a methodical way, pressing each one delicately, with a sweeping motion. She watches him. She wonders whether he knows of her existence. She is thinking of waving a sign, displaying a cryptic message on a placard to tell him that she loves him.

There is another window across the room, a large sash window high above the ground. It lifts open onto a wide sill, where the pushing pecking piggery of pigeons, flashing waves of iridescence, shove and coo and cock their heads to observe her, hoping she'll leave crumbs from the meals brought in to her.

But now one of the pigeons has found its way inside, has hopped from the sill and slipped beneath the frame to the shiny skidding floor. She turns in her chair, but the movement startles the bird and it flies upwards to escape, to crash repeatedly against the glass, flapping in clumsy commotion.

The girl leaps up to assist, but, as she approaches, the pigeon flies from her in a great distressing turmoil of squeaking wings, towards the small square of daylight over her desk. Papers flutter through the rushing air. She hurries back, aware of a strangely intimate, dusty smell as wings brush against her face, panic leaking into the room.

Struggling to unfasten the catch, she happens to glance upwards – to notice the man as he stands up from the bench. As he walks down the path to leave, he watches, moving towards her, as she opens the window, releasing the terror stricken creature into the afternoon.

His eye catches hers as he walks down the path. The man in the white shirt, the panicking pigeon and the young woman battling to open the window; her heart fluttering through the rushing air, struggling to be released, to walk down the path; soft wings smashing against glass in the effort to be set free.

The man with the long hair closing his book, standing up and walking towards her, and the terrified bird thrashing to be freed. Closing his book, neatly, snapping his book shut, and standing up and walking down the path. Glancing upwards to see the eye of a girl, a young woman struggling to open a jammed window, a woman in a little attic room straining to open a window, as wings crash against the glass and a shadow smashes its way into the quivering sighing air.

The Blue Towel
Joy MacKenzie

My husband's defacto is shorter than me. My friends saw them together. They were eager to report that she is slim and shortish with a shiny bob similar to my hairstyle. And my husband was draped all over her. They also said he looked happy.

I've never met my husband's defacto and I have no reason to think ill of her. He didn't desert me for her, or anything like that. I released him. He was surprised, claimed to be devastated, and said he'd never replace me. He did. It took about a year.

Our sons tell me my husband's defacto likes order. That's good for him. She favours the minimalist style. Uncluttered. And she's packed away all our ornaments. I understand this. I'd do the same. I mean, there's a lot of history attached to those knick-knacks: the cloisonné urns from our first trip to Singapore, the jade tree, the gold dragon dogs, the carved fishermen from Bali, the soapstone figures from Mexico. Dust traps. She's right to pack them away.

I made up a list. I was very fair. Three marble eggs for him, two for me. Large blue butterfly batik painting for him. Small green geese for me. Royal Doulton Toby jug for him. (It came from his mother. An antique.)

My husband was confused about the origin of many of our ornaments. "Where did these come from?" I was stunned. "Don't you remember? We visited that porcelain factory in Taipei. We watched them hand painting their faces. You must remember. I was worried we wouldn't get the dolls home safely. I carried them in my hand luggage. You take the marble horse." He was keen on horses.

Our son said his father had an odd collection of ornaments but it looked okay. It had a sort of character. At least it was his. His home.

Strange how when you divvy up the chattels, half of you becomes transplanted to another place.

I gave him all the blue towels. I kept the green ones. One day, after our son had been to his father's for the weekend, I did the laundry. One of the blue towels had returned. I remembered the way my husband would come into the bedroom with a blue towel draped around his middle. How he was so fastidious about drying himself properly. The attention he'd give to each toe. He'd rub his hair vigorously. He had very thick hair. He was quite smug about the fact that he'd never go bald. He'd always throw the towel on the bed where the dampness would seep into the duvet. It used to piss me off.

Now another blue towel has come back. As I said, I've never met my husband's defacto. I feel confused and irritated about these towels. They're good ones. Royal Cannon. I washed and folded them neatly. But I don't want them back. She must realise the blue towels belong to him. Blue is his favourite colour.

The Cinnamon Game
Catherine Chidgey

"Let's play ladies," says Camilla. *"You need a* manicure."

She goes to my bedroom and finds lotion, orange sticks, nail polish. Although I've just moved in, there is no hesitation, no uncertain searching. Camilla always knows what she's doing.

"What do you think of the place? I ask.

"I have never admired stippled ceilings." She takes my hand, dots cool lotion at the base of each nail. "Stippling," she says, massaging my cuticles, "reminds one of cottage cheese."

"It's all right if you don't look up, though."

Camilla admires her own luminous hands, splays them before me like wings. "You," she accuses, "have no moons." She pushes back my dead cuticles with an orange stick. "If you do this every day you'll have moons."

It hurts; I nod, and do not move my hand.

Camilla pulled the scarf tight across my eyes. It was her mother's; a cool, slippery fabric patterned with diamonds. She'd taken it from her parent's dressing table when they were out. Rachel and I had watched from the hall, not daring to enter the room where the pink satin quilt lay crooked on the bed and small piles of stockings and underpants and inside-out socks cluttered the floor.

I squirmed on the high kitchen stool. "You're pulling my hair," I said quietly.

Camilla tied a second knot. "The prisoner is complaining." Rachel giggled.

I heard cupboards opening, lids screwed off jars, water running. Rachel and Camilla stifling occasional laughter.

"You can't," whispered Rachel at one point.

A rattle of plates, jumbled cutlery, knife on a wooden board. Then Camilla and Rachel standing very close to me.

"Can you see?"

I shook my head, forgetting I could talk with my eyes bound.

"Honest?"

I nodded.

"Give her the first one."

My hand was guided to a saucer, my fingertip placed in powder.

"Now taste it."

It was soft, fine; the texture of the scented talcum my mother left sprinkled in the bathroom after a shower. Sometimes you could see her footprints in it.

"Is it — cinnamon?"

"Hmm," said Camilla. "The prisoner has guessed well. The next specimen will be more difficult." I felt a gentle breeze against my face; Camilla fanning instructions to Rachel. Again my finger was guided to the saucer. I caught my breath, snatched my hand away. The substance was slimy. Raw.

"I'm not tasting that," I whispered.

"The prisoner is disobedient," said Camilla. "We shall have to force-feed."

Camilla glances around the room, still jabbing with the orange stick. "We'll have to do something about the soft furnishings," she says firmly. "Salmon drapes, avocado carpet. Cottage cheese ceiling. You're living in a giant sandwich."

"Rachel paid a designer to do it," I say, watching the beginnings of a half-moon rising from my thumbnail. "And it's her house."

Camilla's lips twitch. She shakes the nail polish so rapidly it becomes a blur of ruby. She doesn't say anything, and all I can hear are the mixing beads moving inside the bottle, colliding like tiny stones.

Real Lions
Victoria Feltham

My son's Happy Meal lion is almost tasteful, for a Macdonalds toy. Do I mean realistic? No. The tiny toy is too emasculated and sweet. But the fake fur mane holds its own against our envelope of real lion fur: identical texture and similar colour.

The real fur isn't mane, but hair shaved from the front leg of an elderly zoo lioness with suspected kidney failure.

Forsythe Radiology, where I work, is near the zoo. We often x-ray their sick animals as a favour – chimps and otters, the odd parrot. But she was our first lion, so I brought Frankie down to see her.

She had been anaesthetised at the zoo. They lugged her through the swing doors on a big canvas square, as though she were garden rubbish, then tipped her onto the x-ray table and shaved her leg, so that the radiologist could inject his contrast solution.

Unconscious, she looked like a giant toy herself. Existence seemed to have been surgically removed. Then the zoo vet started pumping on her sternum, people exchanged anxious information about her vital signs, and I realised she might not emerge from the anaesthetic. Frankie, stroking the tawny contents of his envelope, didn't sense anything was wrong. I took him home and we looked up lions.

An *Evening Post* lion escaped from a circus because the youth who was hired just to lock it up after its act failed to secure the cage door.

Oxford Junior Encyclopaedia lions were rather proper. They hunt in groups, but live in monogamous pairs.

Wild Sex lions live in prides. The presiding male is replaced every few years. *Wild Sex* lions copulate repeatedly over a short period, often with the same lioness. Another male may then take over, because lionesses are insatiable.

So where does the second one come from? I shut the book and deflected Frankie to Encarta.

"What's insatiable?" he said.

Encarta male cubs are expelled at three-and-a-half. (So perhaps they skulk on the fringes.) Encarta lions are polygamous, breeding every two years in the wild, once every year in captivity.

Next day I rang the zoo for enlightenment.

The lion expert dismissed *Wild Sex* as sensationalism, and pooh-poohed the *Encyclopaedia* as nineteen-fifties moralising: prides accept one adult male at a time; the new boss kills the former boss's male offspring; other adult males live alone.

"Has the zoo got cubs?" I asked her.

No, just adults: one male, one female. Well, no females now, but they'll borrow some. And no cubs.

"Why? Is the male too old?"

No, there were never any cubs. Captive lions breed voraciously. The female would've produced a cub every year. So the male had a vasectomy.

I got off the phone as fast as I could.

The dead lioness had never bred. Captive and barren. She would've come on heat though. Like any cat.

With only a Happy Meal lion for company.

The Beautiful Long Blue Liberty Silk Scarf
Betty Chambers

You have this terrible hair see. It's thin, it's fine and it's mousy. You have it styled, you have it tinted, permed or cut short, the result is always the same, you still have terrible hair. So you buy a wig. Every time you look in the mirror you nearly fall over with fright, because it seems that Phyllis Diller is looking right back at you.

You have the wig re-styled so often to try to create the real you look that in the end you might as well go back to how you were, because most of the wig has been clipped away and it's hard to tell the difference.

So you are back to where you started, except that you've spent all this money on a wig you can't even sell second hand because no one's buying near bald wigs this season.

Your daughter finds this beautiful long blue Liberty silk scarf at the opportunity shop. She gives it to you, hoping that you might be able to fix it on your head. You can't. You're disappointed. She says keep the scarf anyway.

One night you're watching television, and there's Elizabeth Moody, the actress, demonstrating how she fixes headgear in place with the aid of a pair of old de-legged panty hose and a couple of bobby pins.

You grab some scissors and hack the legs off a perfectly good pair of stockings, pull the pants part onto your head and fix the beautiful long blue Liberty silk scarf in position with two hair clips. You think, Oh Elizabeth Moody, may my blessings on you fall, and you are so happy because the next day you have this business appointment in Hereford Street.

The next day's very windy, see, but you know you're going to look just fine tricked out in your classic blue linen and the beautiful long blue Liberty silk scarf.

You're dressed. You pull the top end of the panty hose onto your head, tuck under the bits that used to have legs, wind round the beautiful long blue Liberty silk scarf and neatly anchor it. Very nice, you say admiringly to your reflection, and off you go for your appointment in Hereford Street.

It's very windy along Hereford Street, but you know your head's neat and tidy. Your business completed, you go back home. You put your car away and you go inside to change. You can't resist having another look in the mirror.

You nearly fall over with shock. It's not Phyllis Diller returned, but a nutter with the butt end of a pair of panty hose on her head, and the bits where the legs used to be are sticking up like horns.

Now you're back along Hereford Street, asking if anyone has found a beautiful long blue Liberty silk scarf; and you're carrying a custard pie, just in case you should happen to meet Elizabeth Moody.

That Summer Out Eeling
Rachael King

If there's one thing that comes back to me about that summer, it's the look on Josh Henderson's face when I caught the eel. Not the sun. Not the feel of the grass on my bare toes as I ran through it – fast – to avoid the prickles. Not the pain in my ankle when I twisted it and nobody believed me.

We kids were always making stuff like that up, always finding some excuse to wear a bandage or a sticking plaster. And that summer, when a whole bunch of kids from our neighbourhood went eeling up the local river with Sam's dad, they laughed at me and left me to trail behind.

Josh started throwing stones at me when Sam's dad wasn't looking. One hit me on the head; not very hard, but I started crying anyway. I sat down. Pretty soon Owen's dad was coming up the rear with some sandwiches he'd made for us all, and he picked me up and gave me a piggy back. Owen's dad was funny. He had a huge beard like a blanket. When we caught up with the others, everyone started pointing at my ankle and when I looked down I saw that it had swollen up and looked very painful. Pink and ugly. I was so proud. I had a real twisted ankle, and all the other kids looked a bit jealous. But not half as jealous as when Sam's dad gave me the gaff and I plunged it into the river and pulled out the blackest, the meanest looking eel you've ever seen. I held it high above my head as the other kids started yelling "throw it!" and I threw it, hook and all. It flew through the air and landed a good three metres away from the river.

When you pull an eel out of the river and onto the grass, it can wriggle right back into the water before you've got a chance to grab it. We used Sam's dad's "scoop" method, cupping our hands to roll it as far away as we could, to where it was safe to try and put it in the sack without losing it.

I had seen the look on Josh Henderson's face. It was a mute and impotent spite, particularly when Owen's dad thumped me on the back and flashed me that beardy smile. Josh fell on the eel, and everyone was chanting "Scoop! Scoop!" at him, and he scooped so hard that ugly old eel went backwards over his head towards me and the river. It landed, slimy and writhing in my lap where I sat on the grass, unable to get up. I screamed and saw its teeth, as it shimmied over my legs, over the bank and disappeared into the water. A disappointed silence. The look on Josh Henderson's face.

Obituary
Rob O'Neill

The same day Michael Hutchence killed himself my cat jumped out the window. Normally that wouldn't be a problem – there were probably hundreds of cats jumping out of windows on that as on every day. But I live in a sixth floor apartment surrounded by very hard concrete.

We never found Pretzel's body, just scratch marks on her favourite windowsill and a little pool of blood below. To be honest, while I didn't like to think about her final plunge, Pretzel was an appalling animal, and if she hadn't jumped I was getting pretty close to topping her myself. In fact, a few months before her demise I had met a vet in a downtown bar and, after she'd told me all about her hard day castrating bulls, I asked her if you needed any reason to get a cat put down.

"Normally," she slurred. "What's wrong with her?"

"Nothing. She's perfectly healthy."

"So why do you want her put down?"

"I don't like her," was the best I could do.

She gave me her card and said she'd do it for sixty bucks, no questions asked.

Pretzel, you see, was the subject of a custody battle when my partner and I split up. I lost.

Pretzel was a zero even by cat standards. She had zero personality. She had fleas. She had a tail that was way too short and back legs that were way too long. Her hair was falling out and she had a skin condition. Her demise became the subject of much joking between me and my flatmate.

"It's funny how you can know someone for so long and not realise they're an INXS fan."

"We should never have bought her that Cat Café — she just couldn't handle the trendy city lifestyle." And so on.

When we first moved into the apartment, we thought having a cat would be kind of cool. We'd been reading Kinky Friedman books and liked to think we had everything but the espresso machine to emulate the Kinster. We were even going to drop our apartment keys to visitors by parachute. But where Kinky could joke about waking up hung over, climbing into the shower and feeling something warm and soft between his toes, the reality for us became increasingly unfunny. The best Pretzel could manage was to throw up on my copy of *Villa Vittoria* — so I guess you could say she was appalling but critical.

In short, the cat was a drag.

I stuck the vet's card over the phone and it hung there, the business card of Damocles, over young Pretz's head — until she decided to take matters into her own hands. When we joked about Pretzel's suicide, people generally disapproved and some even asked whether Pretz had jumped or was she pushed. But while I really did hate that cat's guts, I never would have pushed her out the window.

Not for the sake of sixty bucks.

Honest.

The House Where the Collector Lived
Phill Armstrong

We packed our trestle table and things bought and things unsold into our van, and drove to the house where the collector lived. He had found us in the same way he had found beaked bird skull, lobster frames, dried filament and twig-bodied dragon flies. Built on floor boards rotting close to the ground was this house where the collector lived. A lean-to sun porch each side of the main structure, with flat iron roofing pushed up under the main roof's overhang, was this house where the collector lived. Sills of the junk yard joinery from which lean-to sunporches were built cluttered. Cluttered with flints and quartz, a mummified bat, kauri snail shells, tin plate pressed and cast alloy toys, metal match and cigarette boxes, a tiny wood and paper model of what looked like a funeral barge. Beach-gathered, prickled, parchment-like puffer fish had their place. In the house where the collector lived. And three bricks: "Would you believe," he had said, "these three bricks are as much as 140 years old, they came from a well lining in Dunedin that was sunk that long ago."

He was Maori, not that you could tell, his few genes from another hemisphere overwhelming his birthright pigmentation and blue greying his eyes. His brothers and cousins were, he assured us, penny brown. He was moving back to family and land in the winterless north. So this house of green bevel-back weather sidings, this house where the collector lived, was on the market cheap.

Then visualised myself as a crusty old bachelor, with my books and sherry, walking boots and tobacco, driving to this place in a twenty-year-old jalopy – the very last car built on a chassis, I'd claim.

This is my last port of call, I'd think, this house where a collector lived, and I'd drive a silly bargain that he leave with me the three bricks kilned from the soils of England. That I might creep from my bed in the dead of night and with one brick kill a burglar who invaded the house where a collector once lived. And the collector gathered together some small round boulders, placed them like farm eggs in an ice cream carton and gave them to my wife.

But the thought of me as a crusty old bachelor, killing a burglar with a brick that was once ballast cargo in a ship called the *Emerald*, filled me with superciliousness that both puzzled and annoyed the collector. So to cover my tracks I called the stones Moeraki boulders. He called me Mr Bloody Smart, but added they had indeed come from that district.

Katie Morgan
Tamzin Blair

Katie Morgan sucked. I hated her. She was a bitch. She was a skinny girl with heaps of freckles and a hair cut like a boy's with a rat's tail down the back. I grew up with her. Katie was always on about tits and size and shape and what was rude before anyone else knew about it.

"Ugh, that's rude," she'd say if you sat by a boy on the mat.

"Ugh, boy's germs, no bags," if he accidentally touched her.

Then she would rub his germs on you, and if you didn't immediately rub them off or give them to someone else: "Ugh, Carley likes Garry, Carley likes Gaa-rreey. Carley's got boy's germs."

Katie also had the knack of finding the thing you were most embarrassed about. In standard four she told my best friend she needed a bra. Then she told the class, "Amanda's tits wobble when she runs." Amanda almost died. I was glad I wasn't Amanda.

"What's that on your face?"

"What?" you'd say, feeling like sinking into the ground.

"Aha, you've got a big zit."

And if she caught you looking in the mirror in the girls' changing room: "Man, you're vain."

"Youse are fucken snobs."

"That skirt makes your legs look fat."

But I am moving too fast. It all started in primary school…

I take my togs to school in a colourful, crocheted string bag; when it hasn't got my togs in it it's the perfect size for our fat white ball, which is real leather. Dad pumped it up and put Carley Ward all over it.

Katie reckons our family is rich 'cause I've got a leather ball and a swimming pool and a trampoline and a two-storey house. I know we're not because Mum and Dad are always worrying about money.

Today I have togs in the crocheted bag. Its string makes white scratches on my legs. We walk in a sunny line over to the pool. The sun is in our legs and bags and voices and it is in the concrete. Concrete sun warmth, and I have to miss the cracks because "you-break-your-mother's-back". I balance on a yellow netball court line while Mrs Collins opens the gate.

"OK swimmers, you've got five minutes. If you're not changed, out and lined beside the pool in five..."

Feet on concrete, laughing hurry, bags and pushing. Sun eyes blinking in concrete darkness. The girls' changing shed doesn't have any windows, just a skinny gap between the concrete bricks and the roof. A breath gap. Katie reckons the boys might look through it.

"Don't you care if boys see?" she says, her arms full of bag. She walks into the toilet and locks the door. She comes out with a huge towel wrapped around her and sits on the wooden bar next to my bag. Her skinny shoulders are shivering and her chin is crunched in, holding down the top of the towel. She is waiting for us. She is watching. So I am carefully getting changed under my towel. My knickers are beneath my feet. I try to pick them up and lose the grip on my towel.

"I saw! I saw!" Katie points at me. "I saw Carley's thingy, I saw Carley's thingy," she sings, skipping outside to tell the boys. I go and hide. Mrs Collins finds me later, shivering in the girls' toilets. Wrapped in my towel.

How I hated Katie Morgan.

The Morale Booster
Paddy Griffin

Dear John,

Sorry to have been so long in answering your letter. It had been so ruthlessly censored, I had quite a job trying to work out just where you are.

Things are fairly quiet here, but I'll bet you never have a dull moment in the thick of things where you are. Wish I could be with you. As you take your men into battle, please spare a thought for we who stayed home to protect our country and women and children from the threat of invasion by the new enemy, and the present invasion of our US allies.

I called to see your wife a couple of nights ago and she let me read some of your letters. They're a bit mushy, but then I cannot blame you: Kathy is such a swell girl. Lovely figure and loads of personality; the guys on the construction sites still whistle when she passes. Your brother-in-law dropped in while I was there, he was wearing that suit you bought not long before you left. Kathy had given it to him, as she thought it may be out of fashion by the time you came home. Several other couples arrived, and I'm afraid we got into your cellar again and sent off several more bottles of your favourite vintage. We all offered to chip in, but Kathy wouldn't hear of it; she said you always send extra money to spend how she pleases. She gave me a couple of your classy ties, and one of the guys is going to buy your golf clubs; he has been using them all season anyway.

Kathy is still the life of the party; you should see her doing her Gypsy Rose Lee act! I thought she may have been a little shaken up after the car accident a few weeks ago. You would never know she had been in a head-on collision and written off the Chevvy. It's a shame she had forgotten to keep up the insurance payments. The other guy is still in hospital and threatening to sue. Kathy does not seem in the least worried. She says she can always mortgage the house; it's a good thing you gave her the power of attorney before you left.

Kathy was still going strong when we all said goodnight to her and Bob. I guess you know Bob is rooming at the house now; it is nearer to his work and saves a lot on petrol and lunches. He says Kathy cooks the best bacon and eggs, and can really do things with a steak. I think she may have forgotten to pay the power bill; I overheard her telling Bob something about being a few days late. You don't have to worry though, as you know Bob works for the Power Board.

There is nothing new with me. It's getting late and I had better finish this letter. I can see across the lawn into your front window. Bob and Kathy are having a nightcap; he is wearing that smoking jacket you like so much.

Well, chum, I still wish I was there with you. Have a happy Christmas and give those Ities one for me!

As ever,

Your pal, Harry.

Billy
Gerry Webb

Billy comes down the track.

"Dad says do you wanna come pig hunting?" Impish sing-song voice. I can see a bunch of riders and horses up on the road, dogs milling round.

Bad timing. The late afternoon sun biting like needles and a headache stinging at the temples.

"OK." My face must be a picture of worried doubt.

"I suppose the gelding's across the creek? Dad's waiting."

The river rustles over the gravel, sliding seamless, sparkling. Willie sploshes through in his old boots with the stitching burst open at one heel, and I follow in my sandals. Neill is clucking round his family, hanging washing on a line strung on the fallen puri. He looks soft as butter. Pale and spindly in his singlet and shorts, shoulder length blond hair.

"Whooh boy." Willy slips the reins over the horse's ears and has the bridle on in no time. He's a roan, pepper and salt with a pinkish tinge, a solid chap.

"He's a dog eh, but one thing I'll say about him, Tony, he's easy to catch. You ride him."

I throw myself on, feeling like a nervous boy ordered round by this confident kid. The horse's sunbaked back burns my legs. I get a handhold of mane to brace myself against his stiff-legged stumping down the slope.

Nopera is stretched out on the grass beside the road, leaning on one elbow as if time is nothing. His aquiline nose, with the patch of black scar tissue across the bridge, reminds me of pictures of Indian chiefs. He has his hand cradled round a bottle of Lion Red.

"What's that thing you're on, he he he. Boy, you ride it and give the man the white horse. You got a saddle?

The white horse looks lean and fit. Billy holds it while I throw myself on, to go and get saddled up. The horse jitters, pulling to go. I'll show them. I've never galloped down the slope before, but I let him go. He's in a gallop in a single stride. In a matter of seconds we're nearing the bottom. The reins are too loose, I can't steer, let alone pull him in. We're heading straight for the timber stack. I'm airborne, imagining the broken mess I'll be when I hit the timber. I crash onto the slope just short of it. There's no crunch of broken bones, no resounding snap like a rope breaking. Owch!

Thigh and hip are stinging, but otherwise I'm all right. Billy comes running over, all concern.

"You know, for a moment there I thought you might have broken your glasses."

I look into his genial, apparently guileless face and all I can do is admire the clarity of his freckles. I get tenderly to my feet. The afternoon seems to be in ruins, but Billy is in no doubt that I am simply going to saddle up and carry on. Half-strangled chuckles drift down from the road.

On a Roll
Shirley Duke

We tried to warn her, but she just didn't want to know. She giggled at everything he said, flashed her eyes, her legs and her boobs at him, and within a week they were an item. He kissed her at the Easter Show, pawed her at the Speedway, and took her in a spa pool at Parakai. We heard all about it. Nadine loved queening it over us in the office. She'd have us sitting there, hanging on her every word, munching on our fly cemeteries through all the intimate details. Sure enough, he was staying weekends before the month was over. Nadine's flatmate couldn't understand what she saw in him. He swore too much, smoked too much and drank too much, and he had nothing to say and took all night to say it. "That's the bit I like the best," Nadine drawled.

He and his plants moved in. He gave some to the teens next door and got busted. Then he ran up a huge toll bill, talking to his brother in Aussie. Didn't worry Nadine. "Can't see it lasting forever, he's not sophisticated enough for me, but hey, what the hell, he'll do in the meantime, he's good looking, fantastic in bed and he makes me laugh." She was a bit like him really. More honest, that's all.

He got fired for nicking. Course we all nick a certain amount, management expects it, but he was caught with a whole bootful of the stuff and he'd used her Fiat sports car, very embarrassing. He wrote himself off in the pub that afternoon, reeled home and had a go at her flatmate. Nadine gave him his marching orders that night. He told Ian in packing that the old nipple had finally run dry, it was time to move on. They sunk a few together at the Gluepot and then he asked Nadine out to dinner. He said his luck had finally changed and that he wanted to make it up to her before he left, while he was on a roll.

He hired a suit and took her to a real classy restaurant with live music and everything. He bought her orchids and then gave her a beautiful gold bracelet as a going away present, with an inscription begging her to wait for him. She was touched, well and truly. Just as well cause she paid for it all. She dropped him off at the airport and returned to a totally empty house, stripped right down to the light bulbs.

She didn't know his brother's address. Moved in with me after that. Didn't have anywhere else to go. We got to be pretty good friends. We even did a tour of the South Island together. Mainly to say goodbye – she hadn't seen her family for fifteen years. I'll miss her. She died on Anniversary Day of AIDS. No doubt about it. She'll wait for him all right.

My Mistress
Neva Clarke McKenna

About to leave the office I smile. I smile because already I am visualising my mistress's svelteness. Svelteness, a much prettier word than salicylism or koan, for instance. To roll it off my tongue reminds me of a gazelle, as does my mistress.

I telephone. "Dinner," I say, "then your place or mine?"

"Mine, you fool," my mistress answers. "You know bloody well I won't sleep in your apartment with its thin walls." This is something I like about my mistress, the lack of shillyshallying. If she said such things as "Oh, I don't mind, whichever you like," she probably wouldn't be my mistress.

I put down the receiver and immediately the telephone rings. "Let's not go out and eat crap you pay the earth for," says my mistress. "We'll have an omelette and make love on the rug by the fire. You'd better bring a decent bottle of wine."

A paid slave keeps the grounds of my mistress's home immaculate. The house is one of those places with a stained wooden interior, and at times my mistress has pointed out to me what she sees in the grain on the walls, a tree perhaps, or a child's face, and on one occasion a ballet dancer.

My mistress's taste can only be described as conglomerate. The furniture is a mixture of ancient and modern, in every room are flowers whose names she doesn't know, and on every flat surface a wide range of animals keep watch. There's a goose called Hector the Swoose, a duck called Higgie, a small carved wooden horse given her by an Italian admirer years ago, a row of tiny birds she found somewhere in Portugal, an ugly eastern something, possibly a dragon, left her by a great-aunt, and a green wooden cat with a leery expression.

The omelette is quite wonderful to begin with, but as it cooks we are so busy talking that it flattens. "This always happens," my mistress says by way of an apology. "Thank God you brought the wine."

There is something almost primitive about making love on a rug by an open fire. My mistress teaches drama at a secondary school, and our love-making is delightfully original and abandoned. She doesn't exactly smother me with kisses, but what she does is much more exciting and full of surprises, which I put down to her artistic temperament.

After a time she says, "Let's turn round. My left side's getting burnt. Isn't yours?"

"My right," I say logically. "More wine?"

We laugh a lot as we make love, because my mistress doesn't believe in taking ourselves seriously. Watching her eyes I like what I see, the liveliness and intelligence and joy, and I feel lively and joyful myself and even vaguely intelligent. "My God, this is marvellous," I say.

I call for my mistress to say she finds it marvellous too, but suddenly she points to the ceiling. "Good heavens," she says, "by that rafter there's the head of a beautiful collie dog." She has been looking past my left ear.

Last Exit
Peter Sinclair

I looked down at my father's grave. Its freshness seemed a little indiscreet among the mossier resting places, but it had hardly had time to weather.

Here the sou'wester blows steadily and old pohutukawa amplify the murmurs of the dead. I stood among the tombs and let their brief inscriptions play upon my heart.

Well, *John Sweeney Prendeville, Born Co.Kerry, Ireland, At Peace*, a good long time under the grass, what happened to you? And what calamity swept away the best part of the Grubb family — *Harry P.H. Aged 5 years, Dianthe B., Aged 2 years and 7 months, and Roland, Aged 10 months, Beloved children of J.A. and M.* — in the unseasonable year of 1881? The dreadfully subsided tomb of *Dennis Riley, Died 1893, Aged 22,* tilted its railings in the long grass like a foundering lifeboat. Still down there Dennis? You must have been tall.

I laid my clipboard on his slab and tugged at my father's weeds, but it was getting late and there was really no point. I was about to leave when I saw my old nanny threading her way through the headstones towards me.

She darted up and seized me fiercely by the elbow, a tiny old woman now but still wiry from a lifetime of restraining children as big as she was. "Your poor father!" she said. "I couldn't come, I sent a wreath. Did you see it? Did you like it? Be truthful!"

"It was in perfect taste, Cecily."

"Were you there at the end? Was it easy or hard? I suppose he left you everything? You must be well off now. Be prudent!"

"What brings you here?" I said.

"I came to say hello to your father! I brought him these." She held up a childish bunch of dog-daisies.

"It's thoughtful of you, Cecily."

"Oh, I often come! It's nice and peaceful here. Everyone tucked up and asleep."

The cemetery came to an official end at a low railing not far away, but there were some graves scattered on the other side of it. Here the earth is allowed to harbour the dead as it will, and my nanny pointed vigorously towards the long grass and wildflowers. "That's my spot, see, over there? Nice and green! I shall have bluebells."

"I'm sure you don't have to worry about that for a while yet, Cecily." I gave her the sort of smile permissable in cemeteries.

"You must choose one for yourself! You'll need it sooner than you think. Everyone does! A nice spot, one you'll like. Be judicious!"

"Over there," I said, pointing at random, "near you."

I made a note. It might just be possible to resite the off-ramp a few feet to the left.

When I looked back from the road I could still make out her tiny figure in the twilight bustling round my father's grave, pulling at the weeds and smoothing it down, just as once she'd bustled round the nursery making up my bed.

Cocking a snook at gravity
Patricia Murphy

Amelia Evans slumped on a bench. The sun was scorching, the slight breeze off the sea bringing little relief. And she'd walked down, thinking the exercise would do her good. Huh!

She knew the cause of her misery. Gravity. The force holding the planet together, without which everything and everybody would spin into space. As a child, the idea had terrified her. She'd visualised the farm disappearing into the sky — cows, sheds, tractor ... the lot, and had prayed for gravity to be stronger at the bottom of the world.

Now she reckoned a little less would be a blessing. It was playing hell with her body. It had thinned out her hair and flattened her feet. All points between moved downwards in sagging sadness: bags under eyes, pendulous cheeks, drooping breasts and legs like wrinkled cucumbers.

Then she saw Jean Bickerson. Jean's hair rose in a majestic halo. On slim and shapely legs, she stepped briskly along with Bentley in tow: as if there were no such thing as gravity.

Anger fuelled Amelia's depression. That woman was the same age as herself, what right had she to trip along like a ten-year-old?

She'd spotted her too, "Why, it's Amelia. I'll join you."

When she sat, it was not an "Oh, thank God for a seat" sort of flopping, but a composed lowering of herself. "How very pleasant," she said with an uplifting smile.

Bentley settled on his haunches. Panting from an overheated radiator, he contemplated the harbour. Perhaps, thought Amelia, he'd like to be a ship's dog: Rover or Captain, rather than Bentley. Ridiculous name for a dog, even though the look was right — long, black and sleek.

Jean chatted. Amelia joined the dog in wave watching. The sea sparkled, bottom firmly anchored by gravity, the surface dancing in white-flecked freedom.

Tempting.

Would a dip relieve the ache in her feet? Worth a try. She struggled upright, murmured a "goodbye" and hobbled across the road.

Easing out of her shoes, she moved over sand that was warm and dry, then cool and damp. Soon, foam-edged waves curled round her toes.

Bliss!

She told herself that swimming was like riding a bicycle, once mastered, you had it for life. So, go on ... take the plunge.

Behind her, a voice called her name and a dog barked.

"Sod you," she muttered and launched herself.

Several feet of blue water cushioned her from the dreaded gravity and gave her an incredible buoyancy. She lay on her back and paddled along with the sun warm on her face.

A dolphin-shaped cloud sailed overhead. She waved. "Hey, you're in the wrong element. Come on down."

Something solid nudged her. A black head rose and shook salt water into her face.

What?

Good grief. Bentley!

She laughed. "Giving gravity the paws, are we?"

The dog grinned back, eyes bright with excitement.

Amelia filled her lungs and rolled over. "Right Skipper ... race you to the wharf."

Shearing
Jeanette Galpin

"Come on, Dolly. We got to get finished early tonight!"

Dolly picked up Joe's fleece and brought it to the table. She threw in one easy movement, just as she'd been throwing all day. But this time the ewe fleece failed to arc and open, collapsed in a jumbled heap.

Aunty Moki said "Hell, Dolly!" Aunty Moki's hands flew everywhere – skirting, sorting, discarding. The grease was right up to her elbows. "You feeling tired, Dolly?"

"A bit, Aunty."

She finished sweeping the board and watched them sorting. Angry with herself for being a lousy fleeco, angry with Aunty Moki for pointing the finger. All the anger and all the tiredness tangled together, just like that last fleece.

"Dolly, you know I had to start at the bottom – same as you," Aunty Moki reminded. "Start in the shed as sweepo for the shearers, start in the kitchen doing spuds for the hui. You got to wait a long time before you're ready to work the wool table, do some classing even."

Telling her what to do! It was beginning to rain as they piled into George's ute, crowding under the white canopy. The ute droned up the hill, through the potholes, through the gears, till they were riding high and wide above the river.

In town the picture was a good one. Elvis made love; Joe's hand held Dolly's. She felt his thumb on her wrist, wondered if he was going to put his fingers on her knee, run his hand right up her thigh.

But nothing happened; after Elvis it was all very disappointing.

The others were waiting, singing Presley songs, sorting out rugs to wrap about cold limbs.

"Everybody ready?" roared George.

"Ready!" they screamed back, and George started up with a thundering of revs. Dolly put her head against Joe's shoulder. After a while she slept.

She woke suddenly as the ute slithered sideways; heard George shouting; found herself shivering, frightened, in the middle of the hilltop road — the river roaring on one side, the ute nosed hard into the bank on the other.

And though they tried and tried for ages — revving, pushing — nothing they tried would get the big ute out.

"That was a lucky escape, Dolly," Aunty Moki said as they began to walk in the darkness down the long slope, and on and on along the river road. "Lucky we went into the bank and not into that old river, I reckon. Still, if we'd gone over into Whanganui there'd be a waka waiting there to pick us up. Angels too, and tears from Tongariro to take us to the ocean. No need for paddles when it's high tide up the river."

The rain had stopped; the soft clay oozed between her toes. Lucky all right. She took the strong arm of Aunty Moki and hugged it close. Put out her other hand and grabbed tight hold of Joe.

Moonlight Sonata
Lianne Darby

As was his custom, Louis Davidson seated himself at the piano for his after dinner recital. He had an audience of one, himself; a fine fellow with extraordinary good taste in music and the skill to accommodate. For a moment he pulled himself upright, eyes closed, to smell the sweet, summer evening. Soul filled, he tenderly placed his fingers upon the keys. And began.

The music flowed simply, a touching rendition of "The Air" from Suite in D Major by Bach. Louis was lost, deep within the piece ... when abruptly there tore through the heart of his performance the ripping rasp of Rod Stewart beseeching, *Do you think I'm sexy?* Aghast, Louis froze. Then he rushed to the window, where he discovered a crowd gathering on the patio next door; primitive partying people.

"Philistines!" roared Louis into Rod's racket. He slammed shut the window and seated himself with dignity back at his beloved instrument.

Bach could not cope with such indecorous accompaniment. He began "Anitra's Dance" by Grieg, a gutsy piece. With spirit, Anitra held Rod at bay, but was eventually overwhelmed by the advances of Bob with *Is this love?*. Louis tugged the heavy drapes across the window and shut all the doors. Still the thump intruded, raping the air.

Dvorak sparred with Mick Jagger, Schumann contended with Billy Idol, Debussy, struggling hard, brawled with David Bowie. The masters were being bloodied by the interlopers. Louis was in pain.

This was serious. He hauled out his copy of Beethoven's Sonata No. 17 in D Minor, flipped to the third movement, and attacked the strains of *Spice* sifting through the drapes. Fingers flying, forehead frowning, he dipped and soared over the stiff-faced keys, creating a fearsome rumbling. From outside, swelled the discordant harmony of Queen rendering their *Bohemian Rhapsody*. Louis flung his music to the floor.

Chopin would cope. Chopin knew how to write a decent, note tumbling, chord crashing, chaos of sound. Chopin would drown out that primal, savage beat throbbing through the wall. Louis launched into a vigorous playing of "Fantasie-Impromptu", rolling his head about and grimacing with the agony of it all. Sweat ran down his face, his arms. He was winning ... winning ... the victory was to be Cho...

Jimmy Hendrix. Jimmy wound up to the extremes of the stereo's capabilities. Jimmy, so loud he may well have been throwing his rabid fit while standing in Louis's own lounge.

Louis sat defeated. How could he compete with mega speakers and Super Woofer output? He was being overpowered, not by superior talent, nor finer instruments, but by the giant of technology.

Five kilometres away, on his way home from the pub, a generous bloke contributed his life to the cause and plunged the greater part of suburbia into black silence. All that remained was the breath of the wind and the sparkle of the summer stars...

... and the gentle tune of the "Moonlight Sonata".

Flower Power
Joan Monahan

God, how she hated him. Loathed him for destroying that tree. She groaned in agony as pain ate through her body. The kowhai had been planted on David's birth. He died ten years later.

"Blast Boyd," Mavis said vehemently to the ceiling. "Didn't give a damn about the tree or my illness. Just shot off to a bloody lecture on soils."

Her acrid thoughts turned to earlier retirement plans. Trips abroad, mutual interests. A wonderful life together. First though, improve their house and garden.

"Europe next year," they said.

"Definitely Europe next year," Mavis echoed twelve months later.

"Not yet," Boyd repeated annually.

For the last five years neither mentioned Europe.

His life became garden controlled. At times Mavis imagined the roses laughing, as they seduced him out into rain or heat. She had wept privately when Boyd destroyed her plants and forbade any more involvement.

As pain eased, an idea grew. She gasped at its atrociousness. Wondered if she had the strength. Rising unsteadily from the bed, Mavis took deep breaths to gain control. Slowly her feet shuffled to the door. Then the steps. Finally into the garden shed.

There it was, unimaginably foul. Boyd's drum of homemade fertiliser; a fetid black liquid. Like a frenzied witch, Mavis snatched packets from a shelf, and furiously stirred their contents into the cauldron.

Strength ebbing, she moved outside to rest on a bench. The view of a sky-filled gap, where once the kowhai had spread its branches, renewed the anguish. Slowly the still summer evening calmed her thoughts. A potpourri of roses and lavender thickened the air. Unconsciously she smiled back at a border of bright-faced pansies. The garden was beautiful. One had to admit that.

Mavis shuddered, recalling the day Boyd, in order to create a more spectacular design, had bulldozed beds of shining flowers. He believed in redundancies, restructuring; sacrificing the individual to achieve the final, impressive result.

She saw more clearly the difference between them. She loved each plant, had often bought neglected drooping punnets, then nursed them back to health. Any final colour clash was of little consequence.

Suddenly, absolute horror replaced all bitterness. What devil had invaded her mind? Why, why, why, had she allowed revenge to dictate? She imagined each plant painfully dying after Boyd applied his fertiliser, now laced with poisons. She had only thought of hurting him in the most powerful way she knew. Not a thought given to the plants.

It mustn't happen. Regardless of consequence, she would tell him. Write a note too, in case she slept on his return and did not wake before his early morning garden round. Oh, for the strength to knock over the drum. She shivered at the thought of Boyd's anger.

Mavis sat a little longer before facing the steps. Her eyes closed, head bent downwards. With the final beat of the heart, her life, like a butterfly, drifted out into the garden.

The Sound of One Man Dying
Tracy Farr

Synaesthetes smell music, know numbers by their distinctive colours, letters by music. Gwen couldn't claim that degree of sensitivity, that consistency of sensory overlap. But she did chart her life's passage sensuously.

Childhood smells of freshly-mown grass, of bright new stationery, exercise books covered with brown paper from a never-ending roll, pencils blunt and untouched at either end. It is the colour of hot, wet, red cement drying quickly after summer rain. The periphery of childhood, its fading, is oatmeal (scrub, for the face), batik-patterns, baby oil slick on just-shaved legs, meaty pants from ill-judged periods, heavy with promise and responsibility.

This late childhood sounds like Neil Young and David Bowie, tinny through headphones, overlaid by the surrounding susurrations of the younger ones, the children, storming the library, waiting for the siren. Their giggling is coloured red, like their longing.

Skip to the birthing years, coloured Neapolitan: shit, blood and milk, reeking of burnt toast and plastic wrap. They sound like alone. They smell like a scream.

Gwen had been trying for some months to hear the sound of Alan's death. To smell it, to taste it, to see it. She had thought the colour for it was yellow, for a time, early on. His mother had been disturbed, she could tell that much (she smells upset, Gwen thought at the time), when Gwen wore the old yellow velvet bridesmaid dress to his funeral, but it had seemed so right: the yellow of butter, the soothing feel of the velvet under her hand at the service, its bruised disturbance when she brushed it backwards, her hand running up her belly from crotch to breast, standing at the graveside.

She had decided within days after the funeral, though, that Alan's death had deepened to dark purple. Alan's mother was pleased, as the deep wine purple clothes that Gwen started wearing, then, seemed to her to be much more appropriate for a recent widow. Sombre. A modern kind of black.

The taste of his death was easy: ash mixed to a paste with semen. Try as she might, Gwen couldn't get the gritty, salt taste out of her mouth, from between her teeth, from under her tongue or deep in the back of her throat. It was strongest in the early evenings. She took to gargling with rose water several times a day, as the rose water seemed able to override the dead Alan taste for hours.

But it was the sound of his death that eluded Gwen for the longest time. Perversely, it was only as the sound faded, in the months after Alan's death, to the point of disappearing, that Gwen was able to identify it; it was only as it faded from her ears and mind for the very last time that she pinned it, in a moment of clarity, to its origin: it was the sound of a man, light with love, turning, just asleep, in her bed, by her side.

Aotearoa
Ruth Eastham

He still hadn't come back from the river. Sarah ran her fingertips along the damp wood of the window frame. She had been at him with her fists, and he had gone off down the track, into the wet without his hat. The time before he'd come back; late, hair dripping, silent as the moon. But he had come back. Pray Jesus. She rocked herself on her stool. Pray Jesus.

Sarah pressed her cold palms together. Everything was sodden. She'd not been well. Three months at sea and the baby born on the way. And no news from home yet. Coming here. And no proper midwife. She heard the rain beginning again, little footsteps slapping the nikau thatch. Her sister still hadn't sent those boots she'd written for; the ones she had were nearly worn through. Coming here, to this scratch of a paddock, and the bush on all sides moving in on her.

It would be getting dark soon. The Pattersons up the trail, they had dogs. She could go and ask their help. It would cost some tea, perhaps a pat of butter. Not that she could spare any. Not that those boys needed any more feeding.

"You'll know of course, my dear, that we've had glass now for well over six months."

Sarah remembered when Mrs Patterson had come around and looked that way at the sacks nailed up at the windows. And how would it look, leaving the baby? Besides, he should be back in the time it took to fetch them; back for his supper. Sarah wound the shawl around her shoulders and head, tightening it against her throat. At the door she saw the baby's face, small and white in its cot, looking up at her with astonished, swollen eyes. She stooped to push the sheepskin in closer and went out, into the wind and a gauze of drizzle.

Sarah passed the washing copper slumped against the creek bed, then splashed through the waterlogged spoil of turnip and potato. Further down, the stumps of burnt trees crouched like gravestones, and she had to pick her way through a mess of branches and roots. Now she walked in the murky twilight under the trees, ferns rubbing against her clothes and leaving dark stains, her skirt heavy with its thickening hem of mud. Then it was all around her again, the bush, moving in, moving in on her.

The gorge was close. Sarah could hear the low wail of quick webs of water over rocks. The path steepened near its end. She had to catch at the thin sticks of trees to stop herself slipping. Coming here, she thought, and her boots nearly worn through. The rattle of the river was in her head, stones being shaken in a glass jar. She was standing close to the edge, on the edge of the breaking water, with the mist of the river sweeping below her, a howling child, calling her down.

From the Dead Letter Office
Olwyn Stewart

Veronica's father was in a coma, and there were no planes for three days. People slept, wept and made overtures to strangers. The airport stank of sweat.

She smoked cigarettes, drank coffee from a vending machine and sat on a suitcase with her eyes closed. She said the rosary on her fingers inside her pocket, abandoning words, forgetting to count. Her body felt like a mist with a faint electric charge running through it, so remote a couple of kids stuck their faces into hers and pulled at her hair and eyelids.

There were 2000 passengers on standby.

Despite her prayers, God kept his nose out of it. When the flights resumed she had to throw a public tantrum to get a place on one.

She kissed her father's cold cheek. His body was a waxwork in a coffin, to be draped with a flag onto which old men would drop poppies while her brother recited the ode.

Death was a big distillery in the sky, filtering out the clutter of days and nights, bringing things back to their essence. Her father was a pale boy with gambler's eyes, presenting arms. Elsewhere.

Veronica had a husband then, already cold and distant as the moon. By the time her mother was starting to die, on the same day three years later, he was further away still, drifting out toward the Pleiades.

She was leaving on a morning plane, and as a consequence of a domestic spat she stayed all night in the airport. She wasn't alone. There was a fat man asleep on a heap of newspapers, and cleaners with strong legs and green uniforms trundled their buckets across the echoing floor.

She didn't sleep. The airport was deliberately made uncomfortable, to discourage transients.

Night thinned out into dawn, and a Canadian boy appeared next to her to talk for several hours about rock bands, Alberta and politics she couldn't wrap her brain around.

Her mother died slowly. She liked the world better than her father had, and needed to be weaned of it. There were long hot nights of whisky and scrabble which suddenly went quiet and turned into a vigil.

There was a day her mother wore blue, like the sky she was turning into, and sang in a reed-thin voice: *Toora li oora li addidy, singin' toora li oora li ay, singin' toora li oora li addidy, for we're bound for Botany Bay*. There was a morning when her mother opened her eyes, flicked a glance at each of her children, shut them again and died immediately.

Each time Veronica went away to say goodbye to someone dying, she saw New Zealand through an aeroplane window.

It was piercingly green in the middle of a deep blue sea with flecks of white on wave — as distilled and innocent as the dead become.

The Smell of Horses
Sue Matthew

There is a photograph. The little house in the snow. The house and the time my grandparents remembered with happiness in later years. There are other photographs. Betty, a smiling young mother with Mary, new born and nestled in her arms. There is no photograph of the horses.

It was Mary's first spring. The family lived in a two room cottage Bill had built for the school where he taught in the national park. Bill carted their water from the school each evening in milk pails, using a trolley he'd made.

Clumps of flowers grew from the red brown earth and Mary laughed under her curls. Such a good baby, Betty thought, pegging the morning's hard won washing.

Betty fished the wooden pegs from the apron at her waist, while Mary played on the red tartan rug. Everything clear, sharp and lovingly defined, thought Betty.

Among the tussock, manuka, toi toi, low coprosma. Overseen by Ruapehu, the seasons were set sharp apart from one another and every day was an adventure. She peered around the nappies at Mary. With this sun, they'd be dry before her nap. Then the silence moved aside. Thunder? Looking around she continued pegging along the line. Handkerchiefs, Bill's shirts, her own blue night dress and Mary's baby clothes.

The sound of thunder built, strengthened ... and then horses came, moving along the track from the bush. If it had not been for the thunder of her own heart, Betty might have seen their shaggy coats, moulting now the snow had thawed, the long burred manes and tails, the colours of grey and brown, and the pregnant mares running with the herd.

No! They were moving towards Mary. A scream, a prayer all through her body, Oh God, Oh God! If I run, will they startle and trample? Please no, dear God! That long moment of time. The little house, the mountains, the line of wet clothes steaming in the sun. Her hands gripped tight to the washing line. The movement of their bodies passed the little house, while the dust from their hooves lifted from the track to where she stood.

The horses were just as suddenly gone.

Betty ran, crossing that space which had seemed huge while the horses were passing. Mary sat beside a white alpine daisy at the edge of the rug. The horses hadn't touched her. All round her the earth was beaten and marked. Lifting Mary to her face and holding her close to her body, Betty buried her nose in the sweet smell of her baby's neck. Mary wriggled in her arms. The fat pink hands reached into her dark hair. After a long time, Betty's heart quieted along with her breathing and went back to its normal beating.

She could still smell the horses.

Cabin Fever
Frances Cherry

An adventure staying on his yacht surrounded by beautiful scenery and birds. Rowing to the shore over clear water and trudging along muddy tracks through the bush. And then the rain. Day after day being stuck in the bowels of this bloody yacht inches away from him, feeling as if she's in a depressing little hell hole in suburbia.

With the sun she emerges into the light again. Birds flitting and swooping across the glistening water. She looks across the bay, sees a deer disappearing into the bush, a heron stalking in the wet sand.

As she potters about doing a bit of washing, listening to Brian Edwards on the radio, feeling happy for the first time, she hopes he has drowned. She imagines the hours going by and him not appearing. She could make radio contact, tell Arthur to send help. Then she feels a bump on the other side. Disappointment floods through her as she moves over to help him aboard.

"I've got scallops and mud oysters," he says, as he strips off his wetsuit to reveal his long, thin, pale body.

She turns away, not wanting to see anything else, never wanting to see, even when he gets out of bed in the morning, bending, moving about with nothing on. If she were back at home he could ask what she was doing tomorrow night or the next, and she could say, I'm busy, or, I'll see you Saturday. Here she sees him whether she wants to or not. She doesn't want all this intimacy, can't even go to the lavatory without him hearing; and yet that is the only place to be alone, sitting there, jammed in, knowing if she was any bigger she wouldn't fit at all, putting her head against the dirty plastic curtain and crying silent tears.

"I've kept the fire stoked up," she says, "so you can have your shower."

"Thanks love." He puts his hand on her shoulder as he passes and she feels herself go rigid.

She is watching little terns diving like arrows into the water and coming up with fish, when he comes up on deck with a whisky.

"Hey," he says, looking at her underwear hanging on the railing. "I have to collect all that water; too precious for washing clothes."

"Oh," she says, feeling hurt and foolish. "I wasn't thinking."

"We do our washing in the camping ground at Oban." He disappears inside again to do something to the shellfish.

She picks up her book, is transported to the world of Ruth Park standing on a hill grieving for her dead husband, Darcy Niland. She feels the tears trickle down her cheeks as she sees in her mind that sunshine back street where all the kids played Bar the Door, the smell of freesias, all the people who are gone – Mum, Dad, even Richard, bastard that he was.

She stands, looks down at the water where brown spotties wait.

Rubies
Toni Quinlan

She looked up from her desk in the library and he was there, a stocky man in civvies and a brown belted overcoat, returning a copy of *The Decameron*. It was the voice that attracted her, deep and dark. Welsh.

The first time he took her out they went to a crowded dance hall. A mirrored globe revolved above them, and the orchestra played slow, smoky, sentimental tunes. They danced as one. Did she, whispered the Welshman, nose in her hair, or didn't she? No? Then he must warn her, velvety voiced, it was his duty to warn her, his intentions were strictly dishonourable. He made her laugh.

They took in a movie or two, visited the museum, walked in the parks. The Welshman swung his shoulders and moved with a certain bravado, as though he still marched in the desert. She was not offended when he told her about his ex-wife and other ladies he had known, describing in some detail how pleased they always were to see him. Secure within herself and not completely naive, the librarian took these revelations to be a form of window dressing.

What did he do? He worked for the government, a tedious desk job. Actually he was a broker. A broker? A joke, always broke! Not good, but she laughed with him and was happy.

As winter deepened they met on Saturday evenings after his favoured rugby team had won or lost and went to his room, drank cheap, sweet red wine, rolled up the rug, danced in the darkness cheek to cheek. When the wireless dance programme ended they lay on the bed. Sometimes they took off their clothes. "No," she said, "no, no, no!" The Welshman sighed. He was a patient man.

There came a night when her eyes were closed and her long black hair lay spread on the pillow. He tasted the wine on her lips, nibbled her neck, took hold of her hand, slid a ring on her finger. In surprise and wonderment, she looked. Blood red stones in heavy gold. Where had he found it? He had spent what little he had for her? He loved her? She was touched, felt great tenderness for him, forgot to say no.

In the morning the librarian shivered. The Welshman laughed, puffed out his chest. "The price," he declaimed, "of a virtuous woman ..."

The ring she found to be worthless. In the end she threw it away.

Dozmary Pool
Patricia Donnelly

We had crossed Bodmin Moor to make a stop at the famous Jamaica Inn – which holds no mystery in bright sunshine.

The tour guide herded us off the bus and into the souvenir shop, pointing out the way to the toilets before retiring to the adjacent bar.

But I had noticed the signpost as we turned the corner into the carpark: "Dozmary Pool 1½." My mind was already tuned to the Arthurian legends peculiar to these parts (and if I'd forgotten any, the souvenir shop had glossy booklets enough). Wasn't this the pool out of which the hand, "clothed in white samite, mystic, wonderful", had arisen to take Excalibur as Arthur lay dying?

We were high up on the moor – if I were to venture a little way down the road, perhaps I might get a glimpse of the water. I checked my watch; moving on at 4.30 the guide had said. Time enough for a short stroll at least.

Though I found myself hurrying. The road sloped downward, a narrow country lane, no pavements, but apparently no traffic either. Frustratingly I could never see further ahead than the next bend as unkempt hedges, heavy with May blossom, obscured the view. Almost running now, panicking at the thought of the long climb back against the clock but unable to run, unable to abandon my quest.

The road ended.

A bit of a path led forward through the long sour grass, sedge and rushes. It was the quietest place I have ever experienced. The sun had gone behind the heavy clouds, suggesting twilight. Birds were quiet. Even the water, lapping at the shores of the small lake, made no sound.

I tore my eyes from the scene to glance at my watch – only to find that the hands hadn't moved since last time I looked, in the lane. I knew I had to get back, but still I stood there, entranced.

A slant of setting sunlight glittered on the water; gradually its soft glow bathed the shore where I stood. In turn, the reeds caught the gleam, outlined in gold leaf, like an illuminated manuscript. I dropped to my knees, reaching out to touch them. The gold ran down my fingers, and, as it set, fastened me firmly to the page.

A Clean Slate
Mike Lewis

The moon slid out from behind a cloud, and, just for a moment, the double helix of the Temporal Research Institute reflected a silvery-glow into the night. Matt stopped and held his breath, waiting for the darkness to return. Another cloud blotted out the light, and a grateful sigh escaped his lips as he resumed cutting through the alarm wire.

Two more snips, and the wire was free. He slipped the ends into the feedback circuitry and held his breath once more as he flicked the switch. The switch clicked, and there was silence. Matt breathed again. He carefully placed the electronics on the floor, and then forced open the door.

His footsteps echoed across the dark, empty hangar, and Matt felt eyes were watching him as he walked to the middle where the machine stood. As he approached, the large cylinder gleamed in his torchlight and Matt felt his heart begin to race with excitement. It was actually going to work; he was actually going to go.

They had argued endlessly about who would take the trip. This was to be a direct response to the oppression, and they all wanted the glory of taking part. They had been involved in the past in demonstrations against the minority government, and had marched against the Positive Discrimination Act; but the rest of the group had always drawn the line against anything more violent. Matt had won the argument, his military training counting in his favour. Some prize though, a one way trip through time. But this was a chance to wipe the slate clean, to give a proper start to the country that he and Alex and their friends still loved and still believed in.

The cylinder slid open, and Matt stepped inside, putting his pack on the floor. He pulled a piece of paper from a breast pocket, and compared the diagram it bore with the console before him. He followed the sequence of instructions and sat back in the seat, satisfied. Crossing himself, Matt pulled a lever and waited as the building around him faded and the past came rushing to meet him.

There was a gentle jolt, and he slid open the cylinder door and stepped outside. A cool breeze played over him, and the sun blazed from a blue sky. He stood for a moment, trying to remember when he had last seen such a clear sky and such a perfect day. Rolling vegetation stretched away to the edge of a forest, where tall straight trees seemed to rear up to touch the sky. This is what the country should be like, and what it could be again with his help.

He picked up his pack and slung it over one shoulder, grunting slightly with the weight. The weapons he had brought with him were not light, but the torpedoes were guaranteed to destroy everything within fifty metres of the point of impact, and he was carrying seven of them.

One for each canoe.

The Eel
Anna Gehrke

Cutting through the under-bush, we hear a sound. Whimpering, a forgotten baby, a lost soul. "A puppy!" Down the bank, must be stuck, we have to help it.

The trees thin out, the edge. Below, the slow brown sides of the Waikato tangled deep with willow roots and weed. The crying gets more desperate. We can't see it, but it needs us. "Hold on, we're coming!"

I am braver, I go first. Halfway, handholds run out, so I slide, fingers trailing lines in too-soft sand. Splash-land in thigh deep water, feet sink into silky mud. Nicky plops down. Plop, plop, bits of cliff. "We can't go back up that way." "I know." A twisty weave of trees fences us on both sides. We face the wide river.

Dog must be stuck somewhere in the willows. Whining has become barking, it knows we are near. It's cold, and I'm not liking the mysterious hard things my toes are finding in the mud. "I'll swim to that log and look for the puppy." A few strokes; it's slimy but solid. But then we hear splash! And splishing, and the barking is carried away by the current. Oh no! "You scared it!" "No I didn't." "Yes you did." We are disappointed. "Hope it makes it to shore."

The sun moves away, it's colder, darker, there's nothing to rescue. My clothes cling wetly. Then Nicky shrieks. "There's something down there!" White face, terror-clenched teeth, slowly she pulls her eyes from mine and looks down. "An eel," she whispers, "circling my legs."

"Just stay still." In control again. "It's far more scared of you than you are of it." Impressed with the adult sound of reason, like my Dad ("if you can get *up* the tree you can get *down*"). But I pull my own feet out of the water, balance wobbly on my bum bones, not sure that I'm not lying.

"Kate, it's not going away." I imagine the sly black thing doing figure-eights around Nicky's legs. Taniwha.

"You've got to swim over here. I can't move, it'll bite me." Minutes (hours) of coaxing. She leaps up and forward, panic churns the water, hauls herself up. Log starts slowly sinking, shit.

And then the eel is there, snaking towards us on the log, towards Nicky, gleamy evil eel eyes.

"Swim!" Out into the river, kick like hell. Plough through. Look back once, splashing must be Nicky. There's a beach. Cut through current, powerful strokes, hands hit sand, safety.

Where's Nicky? The river is smooth, vast, brown. I'm ten years old again and running home.

They search the river, but no Nicky. The second day I go with my brother to look at the divers and boats. I don't mention the eel. It and other secrets are hidden in the river's sunless depths. Turning to head back, something wet and furry touches my hand. A small brown dog. It follows me home.

The Bride
Judy Otto

Robert was here at last.

He smiled up at her. "Take a final look, sweetheart."

Anna, gliding down the ancient steps, cast restless eyes over the stone building, where spongy moss oozed through cracks like pus from an angry sore.

Shuddering, she clutched Robert's arm, solid reassurance that she was leaving. She slipped into the MG's passenger seat, its metallic coat doused with rain, a crisp red apple in a summer shower.

"No regrets?" Robert asked, as he slid the car into gear and away from the building that had never been a home.

Anna shook her head. Wiper blades sliced through rain, allowing her a peek at her future, translucent and sharp, as the MG pounced between iron-jawed gates guarding the estate. "This is what I want."

Her decision irrevocable, she did not look back.

Shivering in the warmth that hummed from the leather dash, she glanced at her childhood sweetheart.

"I thank the Lord – if there is a Good Lord – for you, Robert."

After she had slammed his love in his face all those years ago, she wouldn't have blamed him if he had abandoned her. But during this last year, through covert notes and telephone calls, he had been her lifebuoy in a choppy sea.

He placed his palm over her chilled hand. "When I said I would always be here, I meant it, Anna."

"Wasted years." She winced as she felt the pressure of his fingers squeeze hers, recoiled as ponderous branches in the narrow lane lashed the armour that sped her towards a new life.

"You're here now, Anna. Nothing else matters."

The ring he slipped on her trembling finger one hour later was similar to the gold band she had faithfully worn these last seven years. This morning she had slid it from her finger, leaving it to rest in the porcelain dish on her bedside table.

Robert rubbed the strip of smooth white skin, a reminder of years of deprivation. Chosen by her in good faith, but so quickly regretted.

Pride had prevented her from admitting her mistake. Until, under her mother's instigation, Robert had called.

Now he was smiling at her.

"This ring is for life, Anna," he murmured, before kissing the wispy gold hair on her crown.

Anna tilted her face to meet his. She smiled into the gentle eyes of her rescuer. "For life," she agreed.

"No longer a Bride of Christ, Anna. But my bride."

Robert's bride. All she ever wanted to be.

The Draper's Daughter
Waiata Dawn Davies

The Draper had been an officer's batman. That Sunday we pretended not to watch as he marched into church, five feet five of King's regs, shoulders square, head up, moustache clipped, squeaking shoes polished. His daughter followed, angular in brown tweed, face hidden beneath her cloche hat. The Draper's baritone soared above congregation and choir: *Yield not to temptation*. His daughter stood silent.

The Minister preached about the rejoicing in Heaven when a stray lamb returns to the fold, emphasised the nobility of forgiveness. The Draper's trim grey head nodded at each point. His daughter's knuckles gripped white around her leather purse.

After church the Draper lingered outside, chatting with the Grocer and the Town Clerk. The daughter walked away up Mansfield Drive, along a footpath golden with fallen leaves, past gardens where scarlet dahlias and bronze chrysanthemums glowed like stained glass in the autumn sunshine. From that Sunday, for twelve years nobody heard Miss Draper speak ...

People asked the Printer if he had saved any copies. There must have been something, a bit — you know — in the book. But the Printer said the Draper had stood over him, watching him dismantle the type. The Draper then took all fifty copies of his daughter's book and burned them in the furnace at the Borough Council offices.

The Headmaster's wife said the Draper was right. The daughter did not work, merely kept house for her father. Young people wanted everything their own way these days. The Bookseller's mother said the whole thing was a tragedy. Their writing group would not be the same. The manageress of Cosy Nook Tearooms wondered if the book had anything to do with the fact that during the war Miss Draper had twice been seen talking to an American soldier.

When the Mayor dined at the Draper's house his host carved elegant slices of pink lamb onto Royal Doulton plates. The daughter passed vegetable dishes heaped with potatoes, carrots, brussels sprouts. She served steaming apple pie with thick cream in a crystal jug. After bringing in a trolley loaded with tea, hot water and her mother's bone china cups, Miss Draper left the men to their tea and cigars. She did not speak.

Eventually the Draper died. The RSA ladies' auxiliary served afternoon tea in the clubrooms, whispered about Miss Draper's scandalous behaviour. She had refused to attend the funeral but offered to send champagne.

Later Miss Draper was seen at the borough tip, seagulls wheeling above her as she poured a canister of grey dust over empty cans and discarded tyres.

The following Sunday Miss Draper walked alone to the family pew. She wore a dress of flowery silk, a hat of lacy white straw; her hair was cut in a feathery bob. Her voice soared, clear and tuneful, to join sopranos in the choir: *Rejoice my heart*.

Final Peace
Alison Duffy

A city street by night; bright, clean and empty. No sound either, now the rain has stopped. It is perhaps three in the morning. He walks alone in the quiet, past the cafe-restaurant, the jeweller's, the wigmaker's, the patisserie. He has fashioned this street piece by piece. Here he feels safe.

The shine of cars parked in lamplight. A single tree, incandescent with raindrops. Wet tyre-marks, lines of living brilliance, shooting away to the vanishing point. He walks the silent night. There is a tang of frost.

A knock at the door.

"I've brought your tea," she says, putting the feeding cup down on the tray table.

He places another fragment in the puzzle with a sigh of satisfaction.

"Don't let it get cold." She sounds harsher than she intends, can't stand seeing him so intent he hardly speaks any more, hardly looks at her.

"Your tea," she says again, touching his arm. "Your pills."

With a cry he drops the piece he is holding and knocks over the cup. A brown sea laps at the borders of rococo buildings.

"Get out!" he shouts, mopping at the spill with a corner of sheet. Trembling and distressed, she runs from the room, weeping. Down the stairs. These days she hardly knows him.

Domed apartments with curlicued railings on tiny balconies. Columns and marble statues, their graceful limbs gesturing towards heaven. Every detail is fixed in his memory. The city resides in him as much as he in it.

And light, so much light. More than can be accounted for from ornate street lamps or the neon cabaret sign flashing on, off, on, off. Entranced, he walks faster towards the source. A feeling of joy.

So dim now in the bedroom she can scarcely make out his figure hunched over the tray table, muttering, searching the few pieces remaining. His concentration on the picture is total.

She takes the meal away. Says down the phone: "You'd better come."

He stops in the still street to gaze up at the floodlit cathedral, soaring silently into space. At its very top is an emptiness — a hole in the sky where the cross must go. He holds the piece tightly as he starts to climb. Far off he hears voices asking if he has pain, if he is cold...

He has no pain. The ascent is long, up all that light, but effortless. The air growing more and more chill exhilarates. Beyond the cathedral's upper reaches, the starry unclouded sky extends as far as he can see.

"Let us leave him to sleep," they say. "He's peaceful now."

They go downstairs to wait.

Up, up into the clear indigo night. Clinging with one hand to the uppermost structure, he reaches out in triumph to rest the cross in place atop the spire.

The final piece.

Nemesis
Amelia Wichman

In a crowded city restaurant in the droning haze of a Friday night, a man clutched his chest, jerked twice and slumped forward into his steak tartare. From the back of the restaurant a girl half his age fled, pale and fleeting in the stinking gloom of the alley that swallowed her.

Rewind ...

Jessie is as small as can be. It is dark here, but not dark enough. She knows that any second he will see her. Through the crack in the wardrobe door she watches the shadow man eviscerate the room, taking and discarding, picking over their meagre booty in a scavenger's frenzy. Jessie knows her mother is dead; glistening carrion at the feet of the shadow man. Black blood sheens the floor, an oily tide creeping steadily toward Jessie's refuge. The shadow man pauses now, head cocked as though scenting her rank terror. He curses and lurches across the room, slashed by stray shafts of streetlight, and Jessie sees the coiled horror riding his hairless scalp. Then he is gone; the city roars in the open front door and Jessie begins to scream.

Play ...

Jessie grew up. The dull thuds of her mother's death blows marked time. Escaping the cautious kindness of her foster home at eighteen she moved back to the light and shade of the teeming city. Through its faceless rabble she burrowed, as though she too had somewhere to go. She found a job in a glossy downtown brasserie, a home in a small dim apartment, solace in books and the cloak of anonymity that fit her better than her own skin. At night a snarling black dragon chased her through shadowy rooms to a wardrobe with no doors; she woke rigid as it leapt.

A week after she started work in the restaurant a man came in to dine alone. He was greeted with the sycophantic exuberance reserved for regular customers; the maître d' flapped and swooned with the lapdog acquiescence Jessie had come to loathe, seating the man in the window and divesting him of hat and coat. A glass of champagne was thrust at Jessie; she traversed the room with trepidation, already shamed.

"With compliments, sir."

He turned with a smile.

Pause ...

The man is bald. Trapped and fading in his skin, the dragon writhes a dusty grey across his temple to his nape and breathes impotent fire down his neck and beyond. Through a tunnel Jessie feels the champagne splash its frosty blush down her leg; the man curses, and the sound is fourteen years old.

Play ...

The rest was easy. Jessie had rats in her apartment. Stiff furry corpses greeted her each morning when she arose from her dreamless somnolence. She waited, night after night passing in the tinkling glow of the restaurant, the vial nestled in her apron pocket. Her feet ached, but the percussive tones of her mother's murder waned to a heartbeat. He would return.

The Kiwi Contingent
Jim Jones

The ninety-third woman into space was also the first New Zealander. Kate Charteris was a soil scientist with the first colonising mission to Mars. She lived in Utopia Planitia for two years under conditions of incredible hardship, diligently taking samples of the thin red dust. One day, a robot digger she was directing broke through the crust, toppled, and crushed her. So there was never much of a Kiwi contingent there.

By the time of the precious metals boom in the asteroids, a sizeable number of Kiwis had filtered out into space, taken on by the big combines on the strength of their engineering knowledge, or starting up in a small way by themselves. The big metals smelters were on the Moon by then, and if you were in one of the lunar bases on business you were sure to hear those flattened vowels and rising terminals off in a corner of some bar, downing a few cold ones and discussing iridium futures or the AB's chances against Nike or the Pepsi Panthers. And if you made it to Europa, you'd find Kai Tahu fishing the frozen oceans.

When Fleischmann and Himmelmann came up with their equations, the solar system was beginning to feel crowded. There's only so much you can do on Mercury or Pluto, and whenever a few of us got together, it was to talk about the great generation starships that were being planned, to travel for hundreds of years, slower than light, to the planets of the nearest stars. You'd never step onto those planets, but your great-great-grandchildren might. Fleischmann and Himmelmann changed all that, and soon you could jump from star to star like sheep over a gate.

So those of us with money or the know-how boarded the new

ships and took off. You'll find us all over now: skimming Epsilon Eridani's corona, building the Dyson Sphere round Vega, herding brown dwarfs together to make new suns. And here, at the centre of the galaxy, orbiting the massive black hole that holds the whole thing together. We helped to build the Hub Station, the waypoint for travellers, the base for the next step: to travel between the galaxies.

We've got a bar called Earl's, down on the tenth level, not far from the docking rings. You'll find us there most nights, a mixture of hardened old campaigners like me and new blood straight from Home, who can tell us how the kiwifruit crop is doing in Otago and the latest on the Cook Strait Bubble. There're aliens on the station now — twelve foot tall, five legs, nine eyes, all fluting voices and delicate gestures. Some people say we humans should forget our differences, but the Kiwi contingent down at Earl's has talked it over, and we say: bugger them.

Devilride
Amanda Clow-Hewer

"For Chrissakes hurry up!"

Bubba the bus driver sighed. Success hadn't brought the man in the thousand dollar suit any manners, and the old lady looked close to tears. As she fumbled for her fare, tattooed fingers thrust a ten dollar note into her shabby purse.

"My shout, Grandma ..."

Bubba glared down the bus at the skinhead's retreating back. Damn. They weren't meant to do things like that, it mucked up the system. More bloody work. He focused his thoughts, and the skinhead sat down abruptly.

The suit was waving a bus pass, his voice heavy with sarcasm. "I'd like to get to work before hell freezes over ..."

That'll be the day. Then Bubba saw the cellphone. "You'll have to sit at the back, those things interfere with my console."

"I'll sit where the f ..."

He broke off in mid-sentence as Bubba's eyes suddenly glowed red, blazing with demonic fire. Silent and submissive, the suit walked past the other passengers and sat at the rear.

Bubba relaxed as the customised yellow bus pulled away. Bums on seats meant he was doing his job properly. He glanced in the mirror at the back seat: the shoplifter, the paedophile, the drunk driver, the schoolgirl who drowned kittens — and the suit, a lucky bonus. The skinhead, too fond of using his Doc Martens, had been on today's list, but paying the old lady's bus fare changed all that. Rules were rules.

He patted the console affectionately. *We've done well, old friend.* A small green light began to blink frantically. *I know, I know, you're hungry ...*

He flicked a switch and blinding white light filled the bus. With five exceptions, the passengers froze, temporarily suspended in time. The system demanded protection of the innocent.

But not the guilty. Their terrified screams were followed by the squelching sound of raw flesh being ripped apart, then some enthusiastic chewing – and the obligatory satisfied belch.

Bubba headed to the rear of the bus. An empty back seat wouldn't arouse any suspicion, splattered gobs of blood and guts and bits of regurgitated cellphone might. Thank heaven for Spray n' Wipe.

Later on, at the depot, the supervisor walked past as Bubba was polishing his headlights.

"Good shift?"

Bubba smiled and gave him the thumbs up. *Better than you will ever know.*

"Don't forget to sign out ..."

Job done, Bubba gazed contentedly at the four gleaming halogens which now imprisoned another batch of souls destined to spend eternity trying to read the word Lucas from the wrong side of the glass, as well as suffering the writhing and moaning of a thousand agonising, never-ending tortures. Or something like that, he could never remember the exact wording in the manual.

He signed out – *B L Zeebub*. Time to head home, put his cloven hooves up in front of the fire, and see what the wife had burnt for tea. He'd had a hell of a day.

And with any luck, he'd have a hell of a day tomorrow.

Concentration
Denis Edwards

It was two minutes after midnight when Murray O'Malley died. He was in the back of my ambulance, just as it rose over the top of the Auckland Harbour Bridge and began the roll down to the city. Bernie and I said "Damn." We'd worked hard to try and save him, to get him out of his car and into the ambulance. Actually we had worked really, really, really hard. This was because Murray O'Malley was fat. Seriously big. Tubby. Huge. Obese. Massive. He had mega-poundage wrapped around anything in his body even faintly resembling a bone or muscle.

It took Bernie and me and three firemen, all yelling and heaving and sweating, to get him on the stretcher and another round of the same to get him into the ambulance.

I was especially sad, because I knew him, before he died. Murray O'Malley had taught me English and Geography, and he'd always been on my case because I was never one to concentrate. That was my trouble, he always used to say, I didn't concentrate.

A doctor pronounced Murray O'Malley as no more. We drove him round to the morgue. This would be the last time he was on wheels, our rolling him on his ambulance bed into that scarily clean rook, the one with the steel bed in the middle. The Slab.

Murray O'Malley being so fat meant we would only get one chance, knees deeply bent, to heave him up into the air beside the slab and roll him over on it. Once we got him there he was a police problem. They would check his clothes and possessions, and put him in the fridge. And they hadn't turned up yet! Bernie and I said "Damn" about that too.

We went to the ends of the bed, pulled out the handles, took deep breaths and heaved Murray O'Malley into the air.

Ah, but the police were there. Their voices were on the other side of the divider.

She was saying, "Barry, we are not having sex in the morgue any more. I don't care if it is a reclaiming of life or not! No more sex in the morgue! That's it."

I couldn't help it. I know I shouldn't. I started laughing. So did Bernie.

This was a huge mistake. Murray O'Malley's vast bulk slid off onto the floor. The police people bolted. Gone. Vamoosed.

It left us with Murray O'Malley on the floor. People near double in weight when they are dead, and he was heavy before. Now he was absolutely, totally and completely immobile. It was going to take all night to get this inert mass back on the stretcher and up on the slab. Bernie and I said "Damn" again.

There was something else that made me think of saying something a tad stronger. It was Murray O'Malley's being right after all. He had always told me I would make things much more difficult for myself if I didn't concentrate on what I was supposed to be doing.

Heaven
Nadine LaHatte

It was bad enough being dead, but to be escorted by an angel was intolerable. John Roberts had never believed in angels; in fact he'd pointed out to his wife, who harboured sentimental ideas about angels, that wings demanded such enormous rib cages that they were anatomically impossible.

"This is where we are going," said the angel and pointed to an old wooden church. John remembered attending one like it as a boy. The inside even had the same hard wooden pews and the stained glass windows, the same rigid saints. There was a small organ on which an old lady was playing "Onward Christian Soldiers" very badly.

The angel led him to the front pew and, folding his wings in a very tidy manner, sat down beside him. John stared around at the congregation. They sat stiffly, looking very earnest and self righteous. A minister ponderously mounted the pulpit and announced the text, unfamiliar to John since he had conscientiously avoided churches and anything to do with religion for the past forty years. The minister was a short balding man with a high squeaky voice which faded away at the end of sentences, so destroying their meaning. It did not stop him from droning on at great length, though.

John began to move restlessly around the pew, trying to relieve his boredom. A stern glance from the angel stopped him.

Finally the minister finished and announced the next hymn. But then there were prayers. To his surprise he found himself saying the words. There seemed to be a great many of them, long, long supplications to the Almighty. They seemed to say the same thing over and over till he could have screamed with impatience.

At long last the service ended. The congregation filed out and the angel beckoned, "Follow me." They walked along till they came to another church, similar to the first one. "Come on," said the angel and John reluctantly followed him inside, where another service was just starting. It was the same except that the organ was slightly more out of tune and the minister delivered his sermon as if it were a machine gun, in an unintelligible Scottish dialect. It seemed twice as long as the first and the hymns and prayers three times as long.

John hoped for deliverance at the end of this service, but to his horror the angel drew him onwards to yet another church with interminable prayers and abominable homilies. He began to realise that this was going to keep on happening.

"This is too much," he exploded. "Look, angel, I don't know how I got to heaven when I didn't believe in God or the afterlife or live a Christian life – rather the opposite, in fact – but take my word for it, I can't stand churches or hymns or prayers or awful sermons. They drive me nuts. Believe me, I'd rather be in hell."

"But, my dear fellow," said the angel. "You are."

Shadows
Martha Morseth

I tell him about the shadows, shadowy forms coalescing shadow-ward toward me. The doctor resembles a bassethound. His office is hot and I want to take off the heavy layers of clothing I put on this morning in the cold flat. I say aloud, "I should have taken a bath to get warm. I would have, but the shadowcosity of the room was too weak."

His face looks sorrowful and his basset eyes leach pity. I want to explain, to make him feel happy, so I say, "I mean the sun hadn't come out yet and I needed that contrast to relax. A flat room is threatening, don't you think?" There is no answer. His silence thickens the stillness of the morning light,. Eventually he says, "How long have you been bothered by shadows?"

The sun comes through the window beside him. His face is a series of hillocks, terraced paddies, deep trenches. I become excited. I forget what he has said and answer, "You are the earth. You are the cool afternoon breeze, the evening chill, the morning dew. You are the shadowment of life."

"Talk about the shadows," he says.

I think how to tell him, how to tell him about the shadows that have always been. I try to explain in ancient words but my voice is from the present, inappropriate. "In the beginning the earth was without contrast." The doctor is watching my lips, but I think he is not listening. I continue anyway. "God created the shadows and said that they should go forth and multiply." I stop talking because the sunlight disappears from his window and I feel sad.

"These shadows," he says, "describe them."

I am puzzled. How does one describe indigo stroking a hillside, burnished patterns gliding across polished wood, stark crevices beside a path, damp hollows in a tree, a dappled ceiling in early morning? Finally I reply, "They let me live," I say. "They speak to me."

He is quiet for a time, then asks, "You say they speak. How? What do they say?"

"They sing," I answer. "In the russet of evening hills, in the purity of white curtains, in the velvet of magnolias." I stop. I think I am saying the wrong words.

I watch him write in his notebook. He looks sad again, so I say, "Sunbeams dance in the shafts of gold through my afternoon window. They glide and settle, rise again and swirl." I start to sing a song I learned years ago, "Jesus wants me for a sunbeam," I begin and he lets me sing all the words. I tell him it's a song my mother sang to me.

"Ah, now we are getting somewhere," he says and sits upright, gripping his pen tighter. "Tell me about your mother."

A Fine Line
Louise Wrightson

One morning at sunrise, Tracey drives to the sea. She looks at it for a long time.

The sea looks back calmly, like a wide, blue, reliable eye. A swell gathers in the distance. It is part of the eye — the plump flap of the eyelid. Slowly, the swell becomes a giant wave. As it tips over in a suggestive wink, Tracey feels a twang deep inside as though a guitar string has snapped. She fills a bottle with sea water from a rock pool and drives home.

"A walk by the sea is a real pick me up," says her mother. "Your father and I worry about you, Tracey."

The next day Tracey drives to the sea again. This time the sea is wild and energetic. It roars and spits. It throws dead penguins, plastic bags and bits of broken surfboard at her.

"There there," says Tracey. She buys a blue plastic bucket from the dairy and fills it with sea water. She keeps the bucket in the bathroom and uses the water to rinse her hair. She visits the sea every day, walking for hours along the lacy edge telling it stories and problems. She collects rubbish, shells and seaweed. At night she lies awake worrying about oil spills.

"I love you sea," says Tracey.

"I never thought I'd say this Tracey," says her father, prising paua from the bathtub. "But you should be going to parties and meeting boys."

Tracey puts on a clean pair of jeans, dabs sea water behind each ear and does what she's told.

At a party Tracey meets a boy wearing a T-shirt with the sun on the front and the moon on the back. He walks her home, gazing up at the stars. "Look!" he says. "Did you see that? It's space junk. The sky is full of it. I worry about the planets. I can't sleep. I'm relieved when the junk crashes into the sea."

"I love the sea," says Tracey.

"I love the sky," says the boy.

"This is Dean, Mum and Dad," says Tracey. "We met at a party. I'm going to show him my shell collection." Her parents smile broadly.

"This is Tracey, Mum and Dad," says Dean. "We met at a party. I'm going to show her my star charts." His parents smile broadly.

"Adolescents!" their parents groan.

The next evening at sunset, Tracey and Dean drive to the sea. The waves are crimson and gold. Overhead, a faint fingernail-moon curves around a single star.

They take off their clothes, sneaking curious glances at each other's bumps and hairy bits. They walk into the water and stand solemnly hand in hand.

"This is a test of true love," says Tracey.

"I think I'll do backstroke," says Dean. "That way I can see the satellites."

Swimming slowly at first and then strongly, they strike out together toward the horizon.

Arts Page: An Interview About Bill Manhire's Writing Class
Rae Varcoe

Tell me about Bill Manhire's writing class.
How does Bill Manhire actually teach?

He sort of makes a void.

Avoid or a void?

Yes.

But he can't create a void. Any more than you can clean a vacuum.

You *could* see him as a kind of cranial vacuum cleaner. The modern sort. Not noisy or messy, but one with a central clearing station hidden away in the cellar.

So he's a sort of psychotherapist?

Only in the Hitchcock sense.

Tell me about the void.

Every week I run along to Bill with my little wheelbarrow (as prescribed by Dr Bill Carlos Bills: a damp red wheelbarrow with accompanying white chooks) full of words and tip them into the void. Then I watch to see if they plummet or if some slosh about for a bit.

It's a matter of deadlines then?

I hope not! Some of my lines are quite lively.

How much Bill is in your poems?

$2,690 (including GST).

That's the course fee?

Of course.

Bill looks quite sound.

Yes. He looks like sound.

Do you see much of him?

Neck and head. Wrists and hands. He doesn't go in for that sort of thing, I think.

Not even a rhyming couplet?

No. He's very modern. Post modern even.

Meaning?

It's often defined as self reflexive.

What does self reflexive mean?

To me, it means banging your own knee jerks.

Does he say much?

Yes. We discuss Dunedin in the fifties.

What do you think of the controversy over his being appointed the Te Mata Poet Laureate?

I think it is a very inappropriate title.

Tell me more.

I think he should be the Te Papa Poet Laureate. His thumb print is all over modern New Zealand literature.

Do you think he occupies the same position in New Zealand literature as Poets Laureate Ted Hughes or John Betjeman do in England?

Bill is entirely different from them and from our first New Zealand Poet Laureate, Thomas Bracken.

How?

None of them taught creative writing.

But how does it work?

It doesn't. I do.

You know what I mean.

Not as mean as my critics.

What do your critics say?

They say, "Good on you, Rae," which means they are watching TV. Or they amend my words to express their own thoughts more clearly.

Bill Manhire doesn't seem to have this trouble. In Out The Black Window, *Ralph Hotere seems able to add a dimension to his words.*

Yes. The effect can be even more striking when the artist is both painter and poet, as in my case. My series of found poems from a gastroenterology text, which I have incorporated into my series "Out the Back Passage", is displayed in my study. I have set it to music for a wind quartet augmented by two tubas. I expect you will want to have a preview for this programme.

Well, we seem to have run out of time. Thank you Rae.

Thank you, Brian.

Jumpers
Antonius Papaspiropoulos

The man in charge of the Vertigo department store has asked the customers to clear the floor. Rumour spreads fast through Hosiery: there's a man out on the ledge, he's going to jump.

"Go ahead, jump," one man says through his nose. "I'm not leaving till I get my bratwurst."

People don't do what the Vertigo man wants. They loiter, huddle, jam and obstruct. It's like the summer sales. Customers cram themselves into elevators and stuff the stairwells. Everyone wants a ringside seat.

"It's a long way down, twenty-six floors, he'll break like an egg."

"I've heard that the speed at which you travel, you don't feel a thing."

"What if half way through he changes his mind?"

The Vertigo man has heard it all before. When it comes to falling, everyone's an expert. Everyone, some time, has taken a fall — from a bike, from grace, from love. It's only the distance you plunge that makes the difference. And some of us fall harder than others.

"I'm still falling," the woman with the perfume giveaways whispers to her sampler colleague. "Bastard ran off with my best friend. Now they've got three kids."

The foyer pianist closes the lid to his grand. It clamps shut like the lid of a coffin. He's played Nat King Cole all morning and welcomes the excuse for a break.

The Vertigo man wonders why people can't do as they're told, as he disperses a log-jam of ladies in Oversize.

"Come come, ladies." He clasps his hands. "This is no spectator sport." Knowing full well that it is.

"We want to see him," an assertive one says. "I presume it's a him. The women seldom do."

The Vertigo man is at pains to agree.

There's a wail of sirens and a dog pound of cops.

"Damn Pigs," a bad-tie man mumbles to a thin haberdasher. "He'll jump for sure now."

"He's at his wits' end," says the Vertigo man. It's his job to stop the fall, not pick up the pieces. He blocks the path of two teenage boys.

"Hey mister, get outa the way. No law against watching."

And the Vertigo man must secretly agree.

The fire chief's men assemble in front of the store, plastic replicas of one another.

"They'll melt," says the man in Toys (who's been there years). "There may be heat, but there is no fire."

The firefighters fill a round rubber raft with air.

From his dark, wood-grained office, the store manager watches.

"This could dampen Christmas sales," he says to his intercom. "We must carry on as if nothing has happened."

On the roof there's just the pigeons for company. They form a cooing queue along the ledge. A wingless friend has joined their roost. They stare at him through glassy eyes, make strange smalltalk amongst each other — "who? who? who?"

A sea of heads stare aloft; the jumper happy, strangers all. If he saw someone he knew, he couldn't go through.

The chitchat grows, as acceptance sinks in.

"It's strange, but he has a diver's repose."

"Yes, he's a swimmer, obviously."

"Bronzed and brilliant but swimmers drown."

Anticipation breeds such strange repartee.

The man in charge of Vertigo has a stockpile of phrases which he brandishes in turn.

"You're not alone, we've all been down. There are people who can help you. Life's a precipice. A taut tightrope. It's sometimes hard to see the edge."

On the ground, a black man is crossing a cultural divide.

"I know where he's at," he tells a white man. "Sometimes I looks down and lose myself. So now I always look up."

The Vertigo man looks like Humpty Dumpty. How nice, they've sent someone to fall off with me, the jumper thinks.

"What is it, son?" the Vertigo man asks. "A death in the family, an illness, love?"

The Vertigo man extends a hand and watches for signs, the lowering head, the shoe in space. The pigeons twitch and shuffle their feet.

The jumper smiles, moves to embrace the gargoyle on the building's edge. Looking down, he sees all the King's horses and all the King's men. He sees the circular salvation that is the firefighters' dot. He's a dart staring at a bullseye.

"He looks so beautiful," a pretty girl says. "I would have gone out with him. If only he'd asked."

Once, in Amsterdam, he got caught on a stairway. Didn't know whether he was going up or down. This time the fear has gone.

When he goes, the crowd gasps in time, and suddenly the pigeons have the ledge to themselves again.

He shoots upwards like a human rocket, a suited satellite, clearing the rooftop, ascending the sky. A few seconds later he is gone in the clouds.

The Vertigo man crosses himself, sighs heavily, withdraws slowly from the ledge. He's glad for the opportunity to keep his eyes raised. He's glad some things don't make sense at all.

Some people just refuse to fall. For some, there is no going down at all.

Roses
Tony Chapelle

How right it seemed that they should have zapped their car doors unlocked, this sleek cousin and her husband, before they slid themselves inside and purred back down the pot-holed drive. A raised hand through the tinted windows — nothing so vulgar as a farewell bleat of the horn — and they were gone.

The woman had phoned first, more than a trace of condescension evident in her voice: "Grandmother's letter of instruction was specific that this little tea-set was to go to you, and as Darryl and I were touring, we thought we might as well drop it off. If that suits."

Now the awkward visit was over. They had made rapid excuses for not stopping, the woman's eyes flickering over the kids-and-cat-worn furniture. Amazing to think they shared a common grandmother — if the word "common" could ever be applied to one so apparently exalted as her mother's mother, exiled from memory for thirty years or more.

Inside, she sat at the table, opened the carton, and removed the items from their protective tissue. Bone china. She ran a finger over the delicate ribbing on the cup. Very elegant — very inappropriate.

So long ago. She must have seen her more than once, because she could remember the half-fearful anticipation. Five or six years old, she would have been, that last time. Inside, the house had been cool and quiet, and everywhere, everywhere, there was the same carpet with its swirling brown pattern. Dark, gleaming wood; a clock that sat like a large car on the mantelpiece and whirred a warning before delivering its muffled chimes. Grandmother herself just a voice, and … a brief touch of lips against her forehead, as cool as the house. The voice, the voices, she remembered; and wanting to get away from them and outside into the friendly warmth of the sun.

Memories. She wondered just which were genuine and which were the result of her mother's later, bitter reflections: they'd moved away soon after, to the other end of the country. But the voices, the angry voices, surely they had been real.

She looked again at the tea-set, at the ravishing deep-pink roses that decorated the outside of the cup. Why anything? Why this?

Pink roses. Yes. Outside in the sun that distant day she had brushed against such a rose, heavily scented and velvet-soft against her cheek. She had wanted it, had to have it. She had reached out and grasped ...

Screaming, looking down at the welling bubbles of blood; running inside, her cheeks hot and wet. Yes, it was her grandmother who had soothed her. "Hush," she'd said. "It was just a rose." Sobbing that she hated roses, that it had hurt her and she hated it; looking through tears that made her grandmother's face jump and splinter and hearing the voice again: "I know, I know. So much pain, and from such a pretty thing."

Uncle Lionel Tells the Truth
Gordon McLauchlan

My mother despaired of her brother and Dad was affronted by him, but I loved Uncle Lionel. He swaggered and spoke with a loud voice and seemed certain about everything and frightened of no one. When you're cringing through your early teens, anyone immune to embarrassment is heroic.

I was in trouble at home for what my father, puffing up his piety, called "theft by taking" and then telling lies of denial. I had come upon a new fountain pen, kept it, and then said "someone" had given it to me. As stories go it was unlikely, even by my delusory standards.

I was ashamed, but Uncle Lionel told me not to be so silly. "We all lie," he said. "The trick is to pretend you don't, to do it well and with confidence."

"Do you tell lies?"

"Of course I do, and you should too if you know what's good for you. I lie all the time in the interests of peace and good order. Everyone tells lies, and just as well or we'd be living in social chaos. What matters is the quality of the lies you tell. Mine are decent lies, prudent lies, never mischievous."

"You mean white lies?"

"Good God no. A white lie is no lie at all. It's a sort of metaphor. I mean real, fullblown lies. This modern insistence on telling the horrible truth was started by Freud, like just about every modern misery. Therapists insist on it. In fact, beware of women who tell you no lies. They are vicious trouble-makers.

"The worst truths are the proffered truths, the ones no one asks for, let alone wants. Answering the phone – `I'm sorry my wife can't talk to you at the moment, she's changing her sanitary towels.' Or,

`Dad can't come to the phone because he's on the bog. I can hear him from here'."

Uncle Lionel was a small, quick man with slicked down hair who held his cigarette between his forefinger and thumb and flourished it like a baton as he talked. Unlike Mum and Dad, he never pretended life was too mysterious for the young to understand. He seemed dangerously free.

"God wouldn't want to know the truth," he went on. "I mean if he's halfway decent he must be appalled by what goes on. Imagine sitting up in heaven and having the din of horrible truth from earth ringing in your head all the time. I'll bet he invented lies to save himself from all these pious buggers wanting to confess their grubby little sins.

"Imagine if he had to judge your every action and give you points, sort of lift a card up to ten for everything you did every day."

When I got home, I told Mum and Dad I'd seen Uncle Lionel. She frowned and said: "Take no notice of him. He's so full of himself."

"Yes he is."

"And he's a lying bastard too," said Dad.

"Yes, he is," I said, enthusiastically.

From the centre of the city
Diane Brown

"In the context of this relationship I love you," my lover said.

My best friend does not approve of our relationship. She thinks my lover only wants an artificial garden. Certainly, he likes me living in the city on the edge of a park which can be relied upon to remain green and available throughout the seasons and which he doesn't have to water or weed.

At the book awards dinner I wore my best outfit, a sophisticated mauve silk suit. The publishers and booksellers smiled as if I were a child in pyjamas with my hair brushed and ribboned. Required to sing for the dinner guests before being sent back upstairs to bed, while they partied on.

It's adrenaline let down, said my friend when I cried over the phone. A drama teacher, she told me of the actor who had gone home alone, carrying an Oscar. The same night she attempted suicide. Her substitute lover making no move to stop her.

On my way home from the airport I walked along High St. It was not quite dark. A young man passed me. He was wearing those low slung baggy pants, the ones that require an upward tug every five paces to ensure they do not slip down altogether. Feeling superior, I glanced in his direction. A penis swung out from his jeans. Was it real? It was flesh coloured and large, too large I think to be real. I carried on walking to the fast food restaurant.

By the time I had eaten it was dark. Hearing rapid footsteps behind me I ran up the outside staircase. It was one of those moments where you might freeze, but I found my keys, opened the door and slammed it shut. With the light still off I looked out the lounge window. A man was standing at the bottom of the steps holding a bottle, I think.

No one had left flowers or messages or congratulations. After checking the answer phone I rang my lover. My heart was beating faster than normal. My lover was kind and concerned. He is a little worried I might find someone else to replace him. But not so worried that he offered to drive over. He suggested I check my wardrobe while he waited on the phone. What would he do, I wondered, if someone jumped out. In any case there was no one there. Everything was exactly as I left it.

This is what frightens me most.

Speechless
Wensley Willcox

She wants to be back in the warm arms of her husband; anywhere but here, in this familiar street. After her late flight from Dunedin, it is almost midnight. Georgina knocks tentatively on the door, crossing her fingers no-one in the house will be awake.

The outside lights come on. The door opens. Shadowy figures appear in the hallway.

"Welcome. We were expecting you."

"You'll want to see her, of course. She looks so pretty."

Georgina finds herself ushered into the bedroom. A young woman uncurls herself from Annette's favourite chair in the bay window.

"I'll leave you together," she whispers.

Georgina turns to the still figure in the big bed.

Pretty? she thinks. You'd have laughed at that, old girl. When I saw you last, you joked about having been transformed into a garden gnome, complete with bald head and orange eyes. I told you you were a wicked elf with the determination of a rottweiler; forty-seven years old and in your prime.

"Peaceful, isn't she?"

It is Annette's flatmate.

"I owe you an apology, Georgie. I used to be so jealous of you."

"Jealous?" Georgina thinks she must have misheard.

"I thought you were trying to take Annette away from me."

"Away where?"

"You don't understand? Never mind. I just wanted to tell you I'm sorry. And I needed to say it in front of her."

"Ah, huh."

"We've sat with her all this time, you know. She hasn't had a moment alone. Now the others are making coffee. You go and join them. You'll need to know the arrangements for the funeral tomorrow."

Georgina drags her aching feet out of the bedroom, down the hallway to the living room, where she sinks into a chair.

"Do her ex-husbands know?" she asks.

"Best to leave them out of it," says one.

"And her brothers?"

"... have been in and out," says another.

"They are to be pall bearers with you, Georgie."

"I need to get home for some sleep," mutters Georgina, knowing that sleep is completely out of the question.

"You're welcome to stay."

... and break into this tight circle, which has wrapped itself around Annette, her house, her flatmate?

"Thanks. But I'd better get going."

"Don't forget. Annette said you were to give the oration tomorrow."

Driving home, Georgina is thinking what she will miss most is the stories. Annette's verbal sketches of events and people in her life could be hilarious or heartbreaking. Some of the characters in those stories were at the house tonight. Others will turn up for the funeral tomorrow. Each will secretly treasure a version, crafted especially for them.

What can she possibly say on behalf of them all?

She could hire an orchestra. She will write a poem. Better still, she'll keep driving till she reaches Spirits Bay, stand on the headland to farewell her friend. Tomorrow, someone else will step out of the crowd to make a speech celebrating the life and loves of Annette McGovern.

Don't Look
Gwenyth Perry

"You tricked me."

I stare at the cable car, waiting malevolently at the end of our short uphill train ride.

"You told me it was only a train," my voice rises in horror.

"Vertigo's all in the mind. You can't come to Switzerland without going up a mountain." He is being masterly.

It's a choice between staying stranded on a mountainside or closing my eyes while the cable car sways and my knees crumple. He guides me in to a centre pole.

"Just don't look down."

There's a gut wrenching lurch every time we pass a pylon. I slide down the pole and crouch on the floor behind all the legs. He has to half carry me out, eyes still closed, to buy me a drink in the café at the top.

After a while I stop shaking and admit it's a wonderful view, from safely back on the café verandah. We're in the middle of a panorama of snowy peaks, stretching to blue edged infinity.

Nothing seems to matter any more. This will be the last time I give in to this sudden stranger I fell for several voyages ago.

He persuades me to walk up a path in the centre of the last rise, safely away from the edges. I stay gullible, believing his promises. He picks me wild flowers, tiny colours of perfection. Around a sort of saddle we come to a narrow isthmus where hang gliders are launching with their colourful wings. The land drops to nothing either side.

"I'm not going there," I sink down, earthing myself into the stony ground.

He stands, wistfully, watching the confident athletic figures below fling themselves into space beneath their bright plumage.

"You go. Why not try, should be fun," I kid, urging him on.

He looks doubtful, but others have come up now, taking his arms, telling him how easy it is, how he'll love it.

I watch with glee. Revenge is taken out of my hands. He is harnessed into a framework with vivid blue sails. They take him to the brink, encouraging him. A wheel of birds swerves around the side of the peak, distracting everyone. He looks back at me urgently, hesitating, changing his mind and turning just as a gust of wind fills the taut fabric. The bird squeals are joined by another sound as the sail lifts strongly and he teeters for a millisecond before vanishing over the edge.

There is complete silence. Even the birds are hushed. Everyone pauses, then rushes to look. A red sail further out is drifting in, shouting into space.

Nobody notices as I stand up and walk away, holding a bunch of wild flowers. Half way down I stop, then walk near enough to the edge to scatter the flowers into the void, listening to the cowbells drifting up from the valley on the tranquil air.

Going In
Anita Loni

A little scene, illuminated by my surprise and relief, marks, for an instant, one road by which we slip into another land. It catches my memory like light catches shadow.

Atu was unemployed then. I had a part-time job as a door-to-door interviewer for a market research company. My only interest in this came from curiosity. I, who had not explored so much as a corner of the city, was now paid, in part, to traipse up and down its streets.

Gaining admittance to a house was just a trick, though it required a certain bravado. It was a game I played: I thought of myself as a surprise gift on the doorstep. I wore my shiniest clothes and glittery things in my hair, arranging myself into a personification of the Christmas parcel world inside my head. When I neglected to do this, out of tiredness or boredom, I had fewer takers for my interviews. Otherwise I had a high strike rate.

I was delighted to successfully navigate the entrance. But my enthusiasm was left at the door. It was a source of great embarrassment for me to ask the unashamedly loaded questions at all. They were posed in a format guaranteed to bias the results. Usually the interviewees were required to choose, from a list of brand names, a product that "best fitted" a statement read by me, such as "A fun brand of yoghurt", or "A brand of yoghurt for modern active people". Surprisingly, most people gave serious attention to this task. Only a few rolled their eyes at each ghastly permutation.

One evening I interviewed a man who did not want his identity revealed in the slightest particular. He fascinated me with his unfamiliar harshness and suspicion: things which did not seem paranoid, but which I fancied were the product of centuries of necessity, a long chain of descent. Nameless, he was mysterious, secretive, and almost fantastic. I looked around me and felt the lure and pull of a world (not really his but composed in part of it), close enough to touch, but whose entrances eluded me everywhere.

The rest of the evening went rottenly. I could summon up no more courage to pay for my curiosity on doorsteps. Walking home, it seemed as if that other fantastical world was visible in the shadows, and I was under its spell as the night grew dark. By the time I reached my own door, I was half-convinced that I had really seen something. Turning the key, pushing open the door, I was greeted with such a familiar tableau – Atu eating chicken curry and watching TV, the baby playing with his toys and blocks – that tears rushed to my eyes at once. It was such a little, watchable sight, so cosy and sustainable, that I wished I could enter the door over and over again, and see it with the same relief and safety.

The sweetness of being there was as mysterious as the night outside. Later, I began to understand that the admittance I sought, to that strange country which advances to and retreats from scrutiny, had not eluded me after all.

Towards a Shed at the Bottom of the Garden, the Plum Blossom Shows Pink
Mike Johnson

[Note: All quotes in italics are from Gu Cheng, *Selected Poems*, Renditions Paperbacks, Chinese University of Hong Kong, slightly adapted.]

I'm heading down the zig-zag path for the shed at the bottom of the garden in the hope of writing. You're not really a New Zealand writer unless you have a shed somewhere, and you can't do any proper writing unless you are ensconced in your solitude there, poised over the words, waiting.

Sargeson would be proud of me.

I'm heading down the zig-zag path when a large plump bird flusters the kanuka in front of me, takes wing, and I'm brought to a halt by the boastful spring flight of the male kereru. He stands on his tail in the air, outstretched.

It's not the symbolism of it that gets me, the Pentecostal fire, but its casual beauty, its naturalism.

Then I catch a sight I've been dreading. The famous Chinese poet, Gu Cheng, his mouth drawn back from his teeth, creeping through a ponga forest, axe in hand, stalking the blood of his wife. This unquiet spirit always knows when its dreadful anniversary comes around.

The dark night has provided me dark eyes ...

Here she comes, tripping down the path towards him. She's thinking about her son, her lover, the new life she would make for herself. Perhaps she gets a chance to run a few steps, but she doesn't get the chance to turn around. The manuka blunted axe hacks into the back of her skull.

... but I use them to seek for light.

Through slanting shadows the poet approaches the washing line and runs the chord through his murder's hands. Honeysuckle winds around itself; the child sits in the loquat tree. Shortly, a second corpse swings under a new moon.

Wait until that murderer, love,
brings colourful death

The kereru folds his wings and swoops. Breast feathers plumed, the camouflaged female flies to his side, I follow them across the sweep of the valley into the kahikatea grove. Awkwardly, with a heavy flap of wings, they come into land and settle in side by side.

I head down to the shed, where I think I'll find refuge. I don't want to write any more "the tragic death of the poet, China's most famous poet in exile, of the Misty School ..." The heart's gone out of it; meaning's died. Instead of words I have two corpses. Instead of meaning I have a misty void.

... the world and I have no more in common

And instead of writing, I sit in the corrugated silence of the shed, which is itself a riddle, and feel the heat soak into the tin, trying to take lessons in grace from a clumsy bird and making up the love of God as I go along to reassure myself.

... the dead rarely walk by themselves

The murderer is still at large.

Fantasy for a Sunday in Spring
Isa Moynihan

Rita came in from the bright garden where flowers and birds were rioting in a sunshower. Above the sofa back, her husband's head gleamed in the half-light. Her Sunday husband, relaxed and somnolent, reading the paper while he waited for the overseas sports telecasts. In the corner the box was silent, but alive. Women were talking to a black woman with a microphone. They all laughed together, teeth and hair shining.

Rita perched on the arm of the sofa, turned up the sound. "We play games," a woman is saying, eyes bright. The others nod happily and join in. They speak of dressing, tying up; of spankings; of wigs, heels, mascara, lipstick.

"Cross-dressing," Warren says, startling her. "Did you know that New Zealand has the highest rate of cross-dressing in the world? There was an article about it in today's paper". He doesn't believe a word of it, he says. Not New Zealand. Unless they're counting the rugby dos where the boys dress up as babies or as women with enormous boobs. But that's just normal – not the perverted, faggoty stuff they're talking about here.

Rita wonders why there is such a fuss made about men dressing as women when women can dress in trousers and shirts without causing comment. Unless of course they never wear anything else, cut their hair very short and despise men out loud.

Louisa, daughter to Warren and Rita, lives in the same town but in a different house, with her lover Atma Singh from Amritsar. He has sensual lips, warm fuzzy eyes and a charm so conscious that it is almost an entity in itself.

In the kitchen Rita fills the kettle and switches it on. She gazes through the window at the darkening landscape and thinks about various things. About Warren's bald and gleaming head. About somnolent Sundays. About her daughter and her daughter's lover. His hair is thick and black and shining — and long. Longer even than her own, says her daughter. But in public it must be coiled and hidden beneath the turban. According to Louisa almost everything about Sikhs is sacred. (How exciting that must be.) They're like warriors, Louisa says. Very proud. Very macho.

Gazing and waiting, Rita thinks about making love. Wonders what it has to do with dressing up and playing games. Tries to imagine Warren in a wig and mascara and heels. Giggles. Do New Zealand couples do these things? She's sure none of her friends do. She can't imagine them playing games. Of course she can't imagine them just doing it either. Straight, with no frills. Like Pak n' Save. Which reminds her. She makes a note on the kitchen whiteboard: Tea bags. Coffee beans. Shampoo ...

Thinking of Atma's hair — which she has never seen — her scalp twitches and there is a rush of warmth to regions rarely acknowledged. She is an abandoned woman. Take me, here on the kitchen bench, on the floor — wherever ...

She makes the tea.

Sticking a Pig
Graeme Foster

Yes, you've seen it done. When a kid. Ten, perhaps.

Uncle Andrew's. Biking home from school. You called in, as often, to feed the weaners, scratch their backs, listen to their happy grunts. Not that time though. Phil Morten was there helping your uncle set up a cut down forty-four gallon drum between railway sleepers. Right outside the sow's door. Ready for the scalding.

Not that you knew till Morten went off to get his knife and Uncle Andrew explained, saying how they were sharing the meat. You felt it was you that got stabbed, but hoped your uncle didn't notice.

Morten got back and tipped the squealing sow over using her leg, but he must have stuck her in the lung or windpipe — missed the jugular. The sow — God she squealed — got out of their hold onto her feet, grunting and frothing at the mouth, and wheezing and choking on the air and blood gushing through the gash in her chest.

You thought it was a nightmare. But it went on: her screaming; the two men wrestling her all round the slippery boards of the sty.

You turned for your bike. But you were trapped, staring up into the big branches of the acorn trees overhanging the runs — though it was the panting, grunting sow with her high-pitched squeals each time she was grappled with, that was on your mind. You stuffed your fingers in your ears, but still heard.

You prayed it would stop. But how could you imagine God patching her up like Jesus restoring Lazarus? You couldn't even believe God cared about pigs. Hadn't Jesus sent a whole bunch stampeding over a cliff just to stop one mad man frothing at the mouth and tearing himself to pieces?

And it was too late to stop the kill. Had you tried, the men would likely have laughed. Or told you to hop it. And what good was hopping it going to do? The sow would still have been screaming for as long as it took to die. You had to see it through, know what happened.

When you turned back, Uncle Andrew, trying to stay on his feet, was carefully stepping away. He was white and the wide whites of his eyes were staring not at the sow but the wall. Morten was struggling with her all on his own, sliding through the pig shit, hugging her shoulders, dodging her open mouth to avoid being gashed by her teeth. He was trying to keep her upright now, head down. That way, he shouted, the blood wouldn't get drawn into her lungs, choking her and spoiling the meat. But she wouldn't die.

"It's no good Andy! We'll have to stick her again!" he yelled, letting go the sow to once more get his knife.

You never saw it used again though – Uncle Andrew stood in the road. But you knew it was, for very soon, grunting and wheezing more gently, the sow did die.

After Her Father (After her father died, the world ...)
Alison Wong

After her father died, the world grew a hole. It was shaped just so — like a white silhouette. A slip of cold air. When she got close enough, Jo could almost smell him — not a trace of aftershave or cologne, for her father was a plain man who had no use for extravagance. Jo could smell his skin and his hair, the taste of him when she was six years old, as he bent down to carry her.

Her mother had called him a rock — a man of few words, a man she could rely on. Now a seam in that rock had broken, like Moses bringing forth water.

Jo watched as her mother lay clothes, bags, pillows over his side of the bed: this is his head, here are his shoulders, there are his legs. Her mother would hear him coming out of the shower, walking down the passage behind her.

Jo walked the house of her childhood. She turned corners and there he would be — reading the newspaper, sitting in the La-Z-BOY half-asleep, watching repeats of *Star Trek*. Just before twilight, down on his knees, still weeding the delphiniums.

It was the small things she remembered: a series of photographs in staccato motion, a homegrown video rewound and played at random. The colour red. Her father changing her, his big red hands cracked from so many vegetables — washing and cutting and holding — his big work-worn hands clumsy with her head, her arms sticking out always the wrong way. She had worn her dress — the one with buttons down the front and cats playing fiddles across the red cotton — with the back pressed high against her throat for ten minutes or more (almost forever) waiting for her mother to find her.

Even now when she brushed her hair, she could feel his hands, the heaviness of them, him patting her again on the head – she had been sure she would grow up neckless. She drove home late at night, felt him ferrying her in from the car, tucking her softly into bed.

Her father had chosen cremation: a cardboard box that could have held apples or bananas, anything, but for its size and blankness; his grey-white ashes scattering.

She had always imagined a headstone. Polished granite with gold lettering. His name, village, county, calligraphic mysteries flowing down in Chinese and across in English (because somehow English and Chinese always moved in different directions); solemn words that pronounced that here lay an important man. She imagined a place she could visit. A grave she could sweep like those of her grandfathers. A place she could bring flowers, and speak with him softly.

Words had been spoken. Loudly. Too quickly. And words were left. Unspoken. Jo had almost rung him the night before, but had come home late – after midnight – a night of wine and conversation, a supper taken with friends. This was the way, the way of life and all things: a sequence of opportunities given and lost, lost and forgiven.

Disappearing Act
Richard Brooke

Jonathon Rust sat on a rooftop in a foreign city. Although, if you knew him well and observed the way he hugged the looping parapet, gasping in the night air which was heavy with jasmine and the irksome smell of petrol, then you might describe it as an act of daring. Below him the lights of the city glittered like rubies, and if you listened intently you might hear the shuffling of a thousand slippers from the Heartbreak Mosque.

If you did know Jonathon Rust you might wonder why he was here, on this rooftop. He should be waking, in his normal way, in the bungalow he had shared with his wife of twenty years. But to do that he would have to reverse everything that had happened in the last two days and return to the town by the sea in that insular other country.

The day of his disappearance had started like every other day, with the wind roaring up from the sea. As he crossed from his bedroom to the bathroom, the frayed cord on his robe dangling, he waited for the creak in the floorboard, as he always did. The mournful face staring back at him from the mirror must have been his own. His clothes felt musty as he put on his jacket. Something in him seemed to shrink away. His fingers struggled with the tie. How many times had he knotted it just this way? "Try a Windsor knot," she said to him that morning, or was it, "Don't do a Windsor"?

Driving down the valley road, Rust squinted though the weak sunlight, listening to the familiar sound of his tyres on the road. Were the trees really leaning over at more of an angle this morning?

As he neared the outskirts of the town he heard the children's voices, the deliberate clicking of seatbelts, and on the corner outside the school that dark-haired young mother flashed him a quick smile as she ushered her small child through the gates.

Rust stopped at the lights on Discovery Drive and found he couldn't drive on. He sat there in his moderately expensive car and thought about the oddities of modern urban life. He began to recall stories of men (it always seemed to be men in these stories, men and cars) who had vanished without trace. Typically, one of these men would head off to work one morning and never arrive. Later a car would be found, parked neatly at the side of the road, doors locked, alarm set. The driver was never seen again. These details seldom varied.

Rust drove away from work and down towards the sea. He looked out across the harbour at the waves receding into the distance. If he had been a mathematician, he would have seen his life narrowing down to a single point on a familiar line. It was then that he decided that he would do it. He would also disappear.

So Jonathon Rust had come half way round the world and climbed the several flights of narrow stairs to the rooftop of this old, crumbling building. The strange city with its unpronounceable name spread before him like a worn carpet. He let go the parapet and stood in the night with no support, soft tropical breezes in his hair. He walked to the edge of the rooftop, his breath coming in gulps.

"I'm free," he shouted.

Yet there was something familiar about the ache starting behind his eyes. He was sweating. He was terrified of heights. Rust grabbed at the flaking masonry of a chimney and stopped quite still. It was the shock, having to admit something now that he had really always known, something he had carried around inside him like an incurable disease. That all you're left with in the end is yourself.

When
Frith Williams

When I was one, people didn't say much but made big eyes and squeezed beads of noise from their lips that scattered across the room.

When I was two, they said, "One day she'll be beautiful."

When I was three, someone said, "Not in front of the children."

When I was four, I said I loved Kevin and changed kindies when he did.

When I was five, Mr Perkins said what a wondrous sandwich I had and did I make it all by myself? And I looked down and couldn't hide the smile in the neck of my jersey and whispered, "Yes."

When I was six the teacher said, "*Angus!*" and threw a duster at him and it hit me in the head.

When I was seven, Mr Perkins said, "My, what lovely big eyes you have," and the wolf butted in with, "All the better to see you with."

When I was seven, my brother said I had a big bum.

When I was eight, the teacher stood on a chair in the front of the class, turned bright crimson and said, "I'm going to throw a wobbly," staring right through me for at least three seconds.

When I was nine, I overheard my sister and brother saying they didn't like me and let's gang up, and I ran away from home with the dog for two whole hours in the dark.

When I was ten, the teacher said that if anything happened to Anna when she had her appendix out, it would be my fault.

When I was ten, I said I had a hundred horses and some of the girls believed me.

When I was eleven, Virginia told me that Greg (who nobody liked) wanted to go around with me.

When I was twelve, five girls called me the teacher's pet through the cubicle wall while I tried to flush myself down the toilet.

When I was thirteen, my parents said I should buck up my ideas.

When I was fourteen, I said, "Why?"

When I was fifteen, things were said.

When I was sixteen, I didn't say no, even though I wanted to.

Now there are children. I make them peanut butter sandwiches and tell them the wolf who sits by their bed at night is really just a dressing gown. I brush bits of city off their knees, watching them run small fingers over the dents left in their skin.

I do my best to say the right things. I say, "One plus one is two." (I do not tell them about quantum theory.) "There, there," I say, "of course so-and-so didn't mean to say such-and-such," and stroke their silver heads — remembering suddenly that the potatoes are still on high. "Never mind," I say, "tomorrow you'll have forgotten, tomorrow is a whole new day."

In the car they ask, "When will we get there? When?" And "Soon," I say, "Soon." So far, this is enough.

It's the Holes You Have to Look Out For
Jon Bridges

The hole in the ceiling gaped like a mouth struggling for air. She had managed to get up there and open the attic hatch, but now she leaned on the bench and stared up. The hole immobilised her as if it were a black spider on the white ceiling, moving leg by leg towards her across the years.

There were no shadows. It was too noon for that. Just iceblock sticks with the sticky paper wrapped around them. One mess for each kid clung to her fingertips as she picked her way back up the beach to the bin. A sharp bit of dried, black seaweed twisted in the sand as she turned to call to the boy.

It had been easy at first. "I'm just borrowing your stepladder, Judy!" Taken a great rush at it, not looking it in the eye as she approached. Set the ladder up on the kitchen floor and climbed up, punching the hatch into the darkness above. But now its great, lidless black eye stared down and she stood frozen against the bench while the stepladder stood there, hands on hips, admonishing her.

"Don't go out over your waist!" she called. The child stood in the water. The smallest waves slipped past his feet then dragged the sand from underneath his toes as he strained exaggeratedly, pretending not to hear his mother. "What, WHAT?"

"Stay near the ..." But the pull of the sea was too great and he turned and skipped until the water came up and tackled him around the knees, slapping his little body into the surf.

In her hand she held the paper from the day after. Of course, someone had cut the picture out to save her seeing it. But she'd kept the hole around it, kept the absence of him, kept it to herself all these years. Now, unreasonably, the simple task of putting that bit of yellow newspaper in the attic, with his matchbox cars and his lunchbox and the rest of his child's things, seemed impossible.

"Just look out for the holes," she'd called with iceblock running down her wrists. She turned and, leg by leg, made for the shade of the pohutukawa and the smooth green curve of the lawn.

The corner of the newspaper had started to soak up some water from the bench, so she pressed it to her T-shirt then folded it back up. She didn't climb the stepladder again that day as the afternoon shadows walked through the kitchen window and across the room.

A Growth Situation
Joan Rosier-Jones

"Simple pleasures for the heavily mortgaged," Garth puffed as they climbed the stairs.

"Don't be facetious," Caroline said.

"It's free, it's warm and while we're here we're saving on electricity at home."

"Don't be crass. This is spiritual. A growth situation."

"Oh Gawd, Caro." They reached the second floor. "Next week it's my turn to choose where we go Saturday night. We'll do something debauched."

The room was full. Some people talked in whispers. Others sat in quiet contemplation of a vase filled with yellow chrysanthemums.

Garth nudged Caroline. "Thank goodness they aren't burning incense."

"Sssshhhh ..."

An Indian in a yellow robe waddled in. The whispering stopped. "It is my joy to be with you," he said softly. "Tonight we experience cosmic consciousness." Garth coughed and Caroline scowled at him again.

The swami stretched out his hands. "We will touch the cosmos. Be aware of every living thing." He plucked a chrysanthemum from the vase and studied it, holding it to his face as a lover might before a kiss. "Never take such perfection for granted." Gently he returned the flower to the vase. "Now breathe deeply, and as we breathe out, we go, aaaaaagh-oooommmmmmm." The sound reverberated around the room, fading in a purr. "Now, together."

Caroline closed her eyes and took a breath. "Aaaaaagh-oooommmmmmm." She was aware of Garth's silence, but soon the communal hum resonated inside, feeling odd but not unpleasant.

"When you are ready," the swami's voice came softly, "open your eyes." The ooommmms died away. "Now," he said, "we will be truly in the presence of a flower. Always in the here and now."

Helpers with baskets of chrysanthemums passed them out. Caroline studied hers intently. She felt drawn into a universe of tiny golden furls. She heard Garth stifle a yawn.

"Now, we meditate again. This time, reach with your heart. Encompass these flowers the world. The person next to you. All the people in the room."

"Aaaaaagh-oooommmmmmmm." The hum glowed inside Caroline. She reached out to her golden chrysanthemum. She encompassed the people in the room. She loved the whole giddy world.

"Ridiculous," Garth declared as they clomped down the stairs.

"What do you know? You didn't even try." Caroline buttoned up her jacket as they reached the outside door. "I know *I* felt something."

Garth looked at his watch. "It's only half-past nine." He laughed. "The problem with free things is, you never get your money's worth."

Caroline glowered. "Be present here and now."

"Thank you, Swami Caro."

They passed a row of potted camellias in the main street. Caroline picked a bloom and examined it.

They didn't speak until they reached the car. Garth started the motor, and Caroline turned to him. "You are so insensitive." Garth laughed again. "Okay, be a cynic. *I* had a mystical experience."

She wound down the window and, as she berated him, absent-mindedly picked the petals off the camellia and scattered them along the empty street.

New Year's Moot
Murray MacLachlan

This year's moot was at the Sign of the Takahe. Afternoon sun shone through leadlight windows on silver service and crisp napery. Caravans and camper vans were parked outside. Balfour, the chief chef, skilfully organised us so by the time we seated ourselves at table no one had done too much and all had done their best. Which is how we like it.

During the entrée, Alex complained fiction was dead.

Palmerston disagreed. "Just because there have been no good books in the last decade doesn't mean no more Shakespeares."

"Odds are against it," said Milton.

"True," I said. "My Phoenix Press is a labour of love, and no one submits fiction nowadays."

"Last year's book was timely," Shirley said. "*A Bibliography of DIY Guides.*"

"Five copies remain; free or swap for grapefruit."

"Fiction's not dead, we're just beyond it somehow," Dobson said.

"No," said Alex, "*Story* expresses the moral order we don't find in life: bad guys come last, loose ends tie up, orphans become kings. Surely we still need to impose moral order on the world?"

"A simple equation," Shirley said. "No moral chaos, no fiction."

I enjoy the moots. Even Census is routine now. Trout was followed by strawberries with home-made ice cream. The Beatles' *Let It Be* played while we got (instant) coffee. Some sang along, others joked about self-service. Conversation flowed.

Collingwood tapped a glass.

"Fellow citizens. Welcome. We'll do the tough reports first: Census and Medical, then a toast, then each person. Now, Census."

I stood. "Same radio report as always. No shortwave anywhere. I'm certain that when we die, so too does the human race. We number sixty-two. Closeburn and Katiki died in June – accidents."

"God rest them," said Collingwood. "Doctor?"

Crom stood. "Today I gave everybody in the world their check-up." ("Same joke every year," Shirley muttered). "There are no new signs of plague. Everyone's as fit as horses. But no one can conceive children; *that* hasn't changed."

"Thanks," Collingwood said. "Please charge your glasses."

("He'll try to cheer us up," Shirley whispered).

"As we all do, I seek to understand how we survived the plague. My answer is, 'courage'. Each day we pledge anew not to offend against our fellows. Our society is not *Lord of the Flies*. Survivalist fiction is vile fantasy. We have mutual respect and personal integrity. Each gives what we can, and takes what we need. Citizens, ours was the first domesticated species on this planet; we remained so during the toughest story in history; now we have transcended ourselves. All the good stories should have happy endings. After everything, ours does.

"The toast is: 'And the whole human race lived happily ever after.' "

We drank.

Notes on Contributors

Phill Armstrong was born in Putaruru in 1934. His early life was spent on the family farm. He completed a plumbing apprenticeship then worked in the King Country and the Bay of Plenty before marrying and returning to Putaruru. There he worked as a builder and in the pulp and paper industry. Now retired, he dabbles in writing.

Cherie Barford was born in 1960, to a German-Samoan mother and a Palagi father, and grew up in West Auckland. The mother of two sons, she is currently a teacher but has worked as a performance poet and has published two collections of poetry. Her poems and stories have appeared in New Zealand magazines and anthologies.

Kate Barker was born in 1970 in Auckland, where she still lives. She has a Diploma in Drama from the University of Auckland and is the author of *Three Bites, You're Out*, a collection of short plays for schools. She is currently involved in writing for the Stella Nova Science Fiction and Fantasy Club in Auckland.

Mabel Barry JP was born in Suva in 1931. Her mother was Samoan, her father Scottish. She attended Leififi Government School in Apia, Wellington Technical College and Victoria University, graduating in 1976 in English Literature and Anthropology. She has published short stories in a variety of magazines. Married with four children, she lives in Wellington.

Rhonda Bartle was born in New Plymouth in 1954 and is living there now. She has been placed in several writing competitions and published in *Takahe* and elsewhere. She has five children aged four to twenty-six. She is a 'mother, lover, gypsy and a writer (at last)'.

Andrew M. Bell was born in Rotorua in 1957. A graduate in Creative Writing and Theatre Arts from Curtin University in Perth,

Australia, he writes poetry, short fiction, non-fiction, stage and screen plays. His plays have been produced in New Zealand and Australia. He currently lives in Wellington.

Tamzin Blair was born in New Plymouth in 1976. She began writing at the age of ten and her first stories were published when she was sixteen. She lives in Northland and is currently working on a novel for young adults.

Peter Bland was born in Yorkshire in 1934 and emigrated to New Zealand in 1954. He has published ten collections of poems, both in New Zealand and England, where his *Selected Poems* has just been published by Carcanet. He was a founding director of Downstage Theatre and won a GOFTA Best Actor Award for his role in the film *Came a Hot Friday*. He now divides his time between Ponsonby and Putney.

Bill Blunt was born in England in 1941 and has lived in Auckland for the past twenty-five years. He has been in the Royal Air Force, an air traffic controller, rubber tapper, dam labourer and reporter, as well as a hobbyist poet for many years. He recently retired due to ill health from his business as a French polisher and furniture restorer.

Jon Bridges was born in Indiana in 1966 and, as a little American, came to live in New Zealand in 1970. He has been a Kiwi ever since. After growing up in Auckland, then Palmerston North, he now lives in Auckland again. He was Massey University's *Chaff* magazine agony aunt for two years. His MA from Massey led smoothly to his sort-of career in comedy and television.

Richard Brooke was born in Christchurch in 1948. He has travelled extensively and worked in Asia. His short stories and articles have been published in New Zealand and overseas. He is currently Head of English at Green Bay High School in Auckland. He lives in Titirangi and "enjoys being at the edge of New Zealand's make-believe city".

Bernard Brown has survived a wet, windy English upbringing (1934-56), riots in Singapore, an arrow wound in New Guinea and more than 3000 Auckland law students. He is of hardy stock — his mother at 96 is the world's oldest active Girl Guide. His latest book of poems is *Surprising the Slug* (Cape Catley, 1996).

David Lyndon Brown's short stories have been published in New Zealand, Canada and the United Kingdom. Many have also been broadcast on National Radio. In 1995 he was awarded the Louis Johnson New Writers Bursary by Creative New Zealand. He works and plays in Auckland.

Diane Brown was born and raised in Auckland and now lives on the North Shore. She tutors ESL, teaches creative writing and reviews books. Her first book, *Before The Divorce We Go To Disneyland* won the New Zealand Society of Authors' Best Book of Poetry Award in 1997, and in the same year she shared the Buddle Findlay Sargeson Fellowship, which enabled her to work on a novel.

Rachel Buchanan was born in Wanganui in 1968, the first of eight children. A journalist by profession, she lives in Melbourne, where she is studying for an arts degree and writing for *The Age* newspaper. She took the Victoria University short story writing course in 1997 and two of her stories have been published in the literary magazine, *Sport*.

Linda Burgess was born in 1948 in Pahiatua and grew up in Taranaki. A BA from Massey University, she is married with a son and a daughter and lives in Palmerston North. She is the author of the novels *Between Friends* and *On the Grapevine*, the short story collection *Remember Me*, and co-author — with Stephen Stratford — of *Safe Sex — an email romance* (1997).

Rachel Bush was born in Christchurch in 1941 and now lives in Nelson, where she teaches English. She has been published in The

Listener and *Sport* and her book of poems and short prose pieces, *The Hungry Woman* was published by Victoria University Press in 1997.

Melissa Cassidy was born in 1969 and grew up in Hastings, Rotorua and Whakatane, where she 'got religion'. After completing a degree and losing religion, she married, lived in Hamilton for five years, then moved to Auckland. "Airport Café" was written 'during one doozy of a marriage break-up.'

Betty Chambers was born in Blenheim in 1919 and trained as a nurse at Wellington Hospital. She married, then became the solo mother of five children. She returned to nursing and later became a potter, a grandmother and a great-grandmother. She recently learned to use a computer and has attended short story writing courses.

Tony Chapelle was born in Rotorua in 1940 and received his education in New Zealand and overseas. A PhD in history, he has spent much of his working life in the Pacific Islands, but now lives in Palmerston North. His articles, short stories and poems have been published in New Zealand and elsewhere.

Frances Cherry was born in Wellington in 1937 and educated unsuccessfully at Wellington East Girls' College. She married, had five children, divorced, fell in love with a woman and now lives blissfully alone in Paekakariki. She has published 'numerous short stories' and two novels.

Catherine Chidgey was born in 1970 and is a Wellingtonian. Her writing has appeared in *Sport*, *Landfall*, The *Listener* and in the anthology *Mutes & Earthquakes*. Her novel *In a Fishbone Church* (VUP, 1998) won the inaugural Adam Foundation Prize in Creative Writing. She is also co-recipient of the Buddle Findlay Sargeson Fellowship for 1998.

Amanda Clow-Hewer was born in England in 1955. A former policewoman, she left London in 1984 and now lives in Northland with her two young children. She always wanted to write but 'took forever to get round to it'. She is a newspaper columnist and the author of *Pan-fried Yellow-Eyed Penguin*, to be published this year by HarperCollins.

Wanda Cowley was born in Auckland in 1924 and grew up in West Auckland and the Bay of Plenty. She is a graduate of the University of Auckland and, encouraged by her children, worked in Tonga for two years. She has published novels for children, short stories, photo articles and poems. Her home is on Waiheke Island.

Lianne Darby was born in 1964 and raised in Auckland. After completing a degree in surveying at Otago University she worked as a surveyor for several years in Rotorua. She now lives in Taranaki where she writes intermittently, between mothering her three young children and milking cows with her sharemilker husband.

Waiata Dawn Davies was born in Levin in 1925. She is the mother of eight sons and is a retired teacher. She is also a performance poet, story teller and author of two books of poetry. Her work has been read on National Radio and the BBC and published in *Quote Unquote* and *Metro* and anthologised in *Penguin New Writing* (1998).

Patricia Donnelly was born in Stockport, England, in 1936 and educated in Manchester and Loughborough. She trained as a librarian before emigrating to New Zealand in 1963. Her first novel, *Feel the Force* (Collins Crime Club) was published in 1993 and she has a collection of poetry due to be published in 1998.

Alison Duffy was born in 1953 and educated in Christchurch. She has taught creative drama in schools and English overseas. She began painting and writing poetry after her son was born and is currently writing stories and plays for radio, and working on a stage play. She lives by the sea on the south Wellington coast.

Shirley Duke was born in Auckland in 1944 and educated at Avondale College. She has worked as an actress, playcentre supervisor, community house organiser, writer and production manager. The mother of three and stepmother of two, she lives in Auckland and is currently dialogue coach for *Shortland Street*.

Denis Edwards was born in Wellington in 1948 and educated there at Marist schools. He has been a policeman, labourer, roughneck, paramedic and an award-winning journalist. Occasionally married. He is also the author of *Vows*, about the Catholic experience in New Zealand, and a book for children, *In League With Jack* (Scholastic, 1998).

Ruth Eastham was born in Lancashire in 1971 and came to New Zealand to teach. She has been involved with the Manawatu Association, Open Learning Centre and women writers' groups in Palmerston North. She is currently working on a volume of short stories.

Michael Easther was born in Tauranga in 1927 and educated in England. After 33 years in general medical practice in Hamilton he retired in 1992. He now practises hypnotherapy, compiles cryptic crosswords for newspapers and magazines, and acts. He co-authored *Christmas Garland* with his wife, Shirley Maddock.

Tracy Farr was born in Melbourne in 1962 and grew up in Perth, Western Australia, where she gained degrees in science and arts. She moved to Wellington in 1996 after living and working for five years in Vancouver, Canada. She now works at Victoria University. *The Sound of One Man Dying* is her first published fiction.

Victoria Feltham was born in Dunedin in 1949 and has a BA (Hons) in Philosophy from Otago University. In 1997 she received an MA in Creative Writing from Victoria University for *Make me*, a discontinuous narrative which includes her previously published and broadcast stories. She lives in Wellington with three of her children.

Sally Fodie was born in Kurow in 1952. She was raised in the Otago high country and attended Waitaki Girls' High School. Now living in Titirangi, Auckland, she leads a colourful life as captain of the Devonport ferry. Her book of humorous anecdotes, *Waitemata Ferry Tales* was published in 1991.

Graeme Foster was born in Te Awamutu in 1944 and was educated locally and at the University of Auckland. He is the author of five books on recreational walks and has also published short stories and poetry. A gardener with an interest in native forest conservation, he lives in Pirongia.

Victoria Frame was born in 1972 and lives in Auckland. She worked as a 'postie' for a number of years before completing a degree and her teaching diploma. She currently teaches at a West Auckland primary school. Her writing has been published in the School Journal.

Jeanette Galpin was born in Wellington. Her best-selling *A Horse of Your Own* was republished in 1992. She has been a runner-up in the Dominion-Sunday Times short story competition and has held a PEN-Stout Writer's Fellowship at Victoria University. She edits local histories and chases sheep in the Rangitikei.

Anna Gehrke was born in England in 1971 and raised in Hamilton. She has a BA in Art History and Feminist Studies from Canterbury University and her non-fiction has been published in university magazines and *Broadsheet*. After travelling overseas extensively for three years she is currently studying to be a sign language interpreter at the Auckland Institute of Technology.

Linda Gill was born in London in 1937. She has an MA (Hons) in French from the University of Auckland and has been a teacher, mother, artist, travel writer and art critic. She is the author of the award-winning book, *Living High* (1983) and edited the *Letters of Frances Hodgkins* (1993).

Trish Gribben was born in Auckland and received her education chiefly by working as a reporter on the *Auckland Star* and raising three sons. She has worked as a magazine editor, freelance journalist and TV researcher/writer/producer. Her books include *Pyjamas Don't Matter*, *Living with HIV* and *Aya's Story*. The latter, with photographs by Jenny Scown, won an AIM Children's Book Award in 1966.

Paddy Griffin was born in Nelson in 1913. His education at Nelson College was interrupted by the Depression and he was apprenticed to a builder. In World War II he served overseas with the RNZAF and on his return became a structural engineer. Now retired to Taradale, Hawkes Bay, he reads history and writes short stories.

Chris Harrison was born in Auckland in 1959. Although he has no formal education in writing, for the last fifteen years he has worked in a variety of creative fields: music, sculptural form and design for the home. He lives in Westmere, Auckland, where he is working on several writing projects.

David Hill was born in Napier in 1942. He has been a teacher, soldier, driver and bartender. In the UK he taught the children of Princess Margaret. He now lives in New Plymouth and is a fulltime writer. His young adult novels have been published in several countries and he also writes fiction and non-fiction for adults.

Daphne de Jong was born in Dargaville in 1939. A former librarian and now a full-time writer, she is a past winner of the Katherine Mansfield Short Story Award. She has published over fifty romantic novels under the names Daphne Clair and Laurey Bright and her books have appeared on mass-market best-seller lists in the United States.

Kevin Ireland was born in Auckland in 1933 and grew up on the North Shore. Today he lives in Devonport. The author of thirteen books of poetry and two novels, his latest books are *Anzac Day* (Hazard Press, 1997) and *The Man Who Never Lived* (Random House, 1997). He is a past president of PEN (NZ), now the New Zealand Society of Authors, and was awarded an OBE for Services to Literature.

Mike Johnson is the author of ten books of poetry and prose, the latest of which is the novel *Dumb Show* (Longacre Press, 1996). A dedicated conservationist and experienced teacher of creative writing, he lives with his family on Waiheke Island.

Jenny Jones was born in Wellington in 1947 and raised in England. Her short stories and articles have been published in New Zealand and England and she has a novel under consideration with a publisher. She is editor of *The New Zealand Author* and a regular book reviewer for *The New Zealand Herald*.

Lloyd Jones was born in Wellington in 1955 and lives there still. A full-time writer and journalist, he is the author of *Biografi: An Albanian Quest*, the novels *Gilmore's Dairy* and *This House Has Three Walls* and the short story collection *Swimming to Australia*. A new novel, *Choo Woo* will be published this year.

Tim Jones was born in Grimsby, England in 1959 and emigrated to New Zealand in 1961. Via Gore High School and Otago University, he crept north to Wellington, where he works as an editor, writer and father. His short fiction and poetry has been published in New Zealand and overseas.

Sheridan Keith was born in Wellington in 1942 and educated at Marsden School and Victoria University. She has published two collections of short fiction, *Shallow Are the Smiles at the Supermarket* and *Animal Passions*. Her novel *Zoology* won the 1996 Montana Award for Fiction. She lives in Auckland.

Rachael King was born in Hamilton in 1970 and grew up in Auckland. She has a BA from the University of Auckland which includes a paper in Creative Writing. She lives in Auckland and works for *Pavement* magazine. Her last published story was in *100 New Zealand Short Short Stories*, but she writes longer stories, too.

Nadine LaHatte was born in Auckland and is half American. She has a BA from the University of Auckland, was once an actor and is now a writer. An official OAP and grandmother, she lives in Mt Roskill, Auckland and has had two books of poetry published by Puriri Press.

Graeme Lay was born in Foxton in 1944, raised in Taranaki and educated in Wellington. He is the author of two novels, three short story collections and the non-fiction books *Passages*, *Pacific New Zealand* and *The Cook Islands*. His latest book is a novel for young adults, *Leaving One-Foot Island* (Mallinson Rendel, 1998).

Mike Lewis was born in England in 1963. He published a computer book and some comedy scripts in the mid-1980s but has recently started writing fiction after attending a short story writing course. Since late 1996 he has worked in Auckland writing computer software.

Cordelia Lockett was born in Salisbury, England, in 1965 and came to New Zealand when she was seven. After attending Auckland, Canterbury and Victoria Universities she became a teacher, but now works part-time as a sexuality educator. She has also reviewed books for The *Listener*.

Anita Loni was born in Wanganui in 1964. She has an MA from the University of Auckland and a seven-year-old son. She lives and works in Grey Lynn, Auckland.

Catherine Mair was born in the homestead on the family farm in Katikati and in 1972 returned there to live with her husband and four children. She enjoys a wide range of interests. In 1996 she was one of the three winners in the Whitireia Poetry Competition and was co-organiser of the Tauranga Poetry Festival in the same year.

Joy MacKenzie was born in Hamilton in 1947. She worked as a postie until she was bitten by a Doberman, an Alsatian and two Pekinese. She has three sons and an MA (Hons) from the University of Auckland. A poet, fiction writer and reviewer, her writing has been anthologised and broadcast. She won the *Sunday Star* short story contest in 1991 and today lives in an apartment on the slopes of Mt Eden.

Neva Clarke McKenna QSM was born and educated in Gisborne. She served in Italy in World War II, then worked in the Prime Minister's office until her marriage. She has published books of short stories, a novel, three historical and travel books and the memoir, *Angel in God's Office* (Tandem Press, 1995). She lives at Coopers Beach.

Murray MacLachlan was born in Auckland in 1963, raised in Dunedin and now lives in Christchurch. He has a BA (Hons) and papers in personnel and quality. His first published fiction was in *Starsongs* (1993), a New Zealand science fiction anthology. He is married to Natalie, collects Wodehouse novels, enjoys rugby, mahjong and rock music and has discovered his birth parents and the men's movement.

Sue Matthew was born in Hamilton in 1963 and lived for years in Taranaki, on the slopes of the Pouakai Ranges, where she recently saw 'the green flash' for the first time. Now living in Wellington, she has a Diploma of Fine Arts and is a graduate of the Whitireia Writing Course. Her short stories and poetry have been published in *Broadsheet*.

John McCrystal was born in Taupo in 1966 but has lived in Auckland most of his life. He was educated at Westlake Boys' High School and the University of Auckland. Currently working as an academic historian, he also writes book reviews, features and academic articles. *Life and Times* is his second published short story.

Jane McKenzie was born in 1955 and raised in South Canterbury. She lived in Sydney for twenty-five years and became deputy editor of *Cosmopolitan*, *Family Circle* and *Harper's Bazaar*. She has a BA (First Class Hons) in English Literature and now tutors at Canterbury University's Journalism School.

Gordon McLauchlan was born in Dunedin in 1931 and educated at eight primary schools in a number of New Zealand towns and at Wellington College. The author of eight non-fiction books, he has also worked in print, radio and television journalism and in public relations. He has previously disguised all his fiction as journalism.

Chris McVeigh QC was born in Christchurch in 1945 and educated at Christ's College and the University of Canterbury. A keen thespian, he was a member of the original cast of the TV series *A Week of It*. He is the father of four daughters and the co-author, with A K Grant, of *Second Wind*, a book about separation in middle-age.

Diana Menefy was born in Christchurch in 1947. She attended school there and trained at the Christchurch Public Hospital. She now lives on a farm in Northland and has three adult children. She has had 'five books, numerous articles and seven short stories' published. Her interests are writing, spinning, old-fashioned roses and photography.

Joan Monahan was born in 1925 in Ponsonby, where she still lives, and educated at Auckland Girls' Grammar school and the University of Auckland (MSc Hons). She was a swimming silver medallist at the 1950 Empire Games. She taught science overseas and in New Zealand. Her current interests are tramping and writing. She celebrated her 70th birthday bungi jumping.

Martha Morseth was born in the United States in 1938 and educated at Minnesota and Pennsylvania Universities. She has lived in Dunedin, where she is Head of English at St Hilda's Collegiate School. Her writing has been published in a variety of New Zealand magazines and literary journals.

Isa Moynihan was born in Ireland and worked as a teacher in England, Singapore and Malaysia before settling in New Zealand, where she obtained a PhD in Applied Linguistics. In 1996 she won the Reed Fiction Award for the short story collection published as *Sex and the Single Mayfly*. She is a full-time writer and fiction editor of *Takahe*. She lives in Christchurch.

Patricia Murphy was born in the United Kingdom. She spent ten years in the Waikato before settling in the Hutt Valley. A BA graduate of Victoria University, she enjoys writing and painting. Her short stories and poems have been published in school journals and other magazines. She won the 'Ripping Good Read' competition in 1997.

Julia Oakley was born in Auckland in 1957, where she was educated predominantly by penguins. Easily bored, at 18 she left for Australia where her free spirit and contempt for office politics saw her work mainly with racehorses. She shuns modern life and lives mostly in Texas, albeit only in her head.

Rob O'Neill was born in Peru in 1959. A close relative of Paddington Bear, he came to New Zealand in 1964. He has had fiction published in *Takahe* and *Snafu*. He is currently the editor of the technology magazine *Bits and Bytes*.

Judith Otto was born in Auckland in 1942 and attended Otahuhu College before starting a secretarial career. Married with two sons, she now lives in Wanaka. She has had several short stories published and is now working on a novel. Her favourite author is Paul Jennings, 'because he makes her laugh'.

Antonius Papaspiropoulos was born in 1962 and was educated at St Paul's Collegiate in Hamilton and the University of Auckland. He spent the 1980s working as a rock musician overseas and since then has been a journalist, press secretary and public relations consultant. His fiction has been published in *Metro*, *North & South* and *Landfall*. He now lives in Seatoun, Wellington.

Judy Parker was born in Echuca, Australia. She has an MA (Hons) and drives tractors to support her full-time writing habit. She is currently doing a second MA in Creative Writing at Victoria University. She is addicted to sunshine, water and ridiculous hats, and is a life class habitué.

Gwenyth Perry was born in Tauranga. A graduate of the University of Auckland, she is married with three adult children and currently lives in Auckland. A Francophile, she enjoys writing and researching in France. Her writing has been published in New Zealand and Singapore.

Janet Peters was born in 1954 in Ranfurly. She has contributed articles to psychology journals and was associate editor of the book *Psychiatry and the Law: Clinical and Legal Issues* (1996). She is a registered psychologist and lives in Auckland.

Toni Quinlan was born in Pukekohe in 1918. She was convent-educated and is a retired secretary, painter and fabric artist. She once travelled as wardrobe mistress with a ballet company. She has won painting awards and has had articles, poems and short stories published. She lives in Whangamata.

Adrienne Rewi was born in Morrinsville in 1952. She attended Te Aroha College and Niue Island High School and in 1970 began a career in journalism. From 1979-90 she worked as a full-time exhibiting artist, then returned to journalism. She has published three non-fiction books, *Architects at Home*, *Fine Cheese* and *Private Views*. She now lives in Christchurch.

Simon Robinson was born in Melbourne in 1970 and grew up in Sydney. In 1994 he left Australia to travel and since 1995 has worked in New Zealand as a correspondent for *Time* magazine. His interests are reading, history, art, film, languages and tramping.

Joan Rosier-Jones was born and educated in Christchurch and has lived in Wellington and London. Now living on Auckland's North Shore, she is the author of four novels and a book on how to write your family's history.

Elspeth Sandys was born in Dunedin and educated at the universities of Otago and Auckland. She has published eight novels, a collection of short stories and has had numerous plays broadcast by National Radio and the BBC. Her latest novel is *Enemy Territory* (Hodder & Stoughton, 1997). She is the 1998 writer-in-residence at Waikato University.

Ellen Shaw submitted the short short story *Pound Dog* and one other story, using that name as the author's and giving her address as 3/38 Barron Street, Waterview. The editor's acceptance letter to that address was returned. The editor has made strenuous but unsuccessful attempts to locate the writer. He would very much like to hear from her.

Tina Shaw was raised on a Waikato farm one mile from Matangi and now lives on Waiheke Island. She has worked in an English pub and got lost in Paris. She read most of her university texts (but avoided Chaucer) and has taken black and white photographs of Auckland fishing boats. She is the author of the novels *Birdie* and *Dreams of America*.

Peter Sinclair was born in Sydney and raised in Christchurch, where he attended Christ's College and the University of Canterbury. Intending to become a journalist, he found his way into radio and television, where he has remained for forty years. He is the author of the novel, *The Frontman* (Penguin, 1992).

Barry Southam was born and educated in Christchurch and now lives on Auckland's North Shore. He has been a film actor, theatre reviewer and addictions counsellor and has published two books of poetry and a collection of short stories. A number of his plays have been produced for stage and radio.

Olwyn Stewart was born in South Australia but now lives in Grey Lynn, Auckland. Her poetry and short stories have appeared in *Sport*, *Printout*, *Tongue In Your Ear* and The *Listener* and have been broadcast by Radio New Zealand. Her short story, *Counting Down*, was a runner-up in the 1997 *Listener* short fiction competition.

Prue Toft was born in 1953 on Auckland's North Shore and graduated from the University of Auckland with a master's degree in anthropology. Her short stories have been published in the *Woman's Weekly* and the *Sunday Star-Times*. She lives in a bach in Browns Bay and works as a equal employment opportunities advisor.

Rae Varcoe spent 1997 writing creatively in Wellington. Now the owner of an MA and a bewildered expression, she has returned to work as a physician at Auckland Hospital. Her prose and poetry has been published in *Takahe* and *New Zealand Books*.

Kaye Vaughan was born in 1949 in Tauranga and left school at 14. She began writing children's stories and poetry in 1996 and short stories for adults in 1997. Highlights of her life include children, dogs, husband, psychotherapy and, at last, "a belief that I have something worthwhile to say".

Sara Vui-Talitu was born in 1972. A Samoan-New Zealander, she has an MA (Hons) in English from the University of Auckland and a postgraduate diploma from Canterbury University. She has been a reporter for Fiji TV and an editor at the University of the South Pacific, in Suva. She is now a PR consultant in West Auckland.

Gerry Webb was born in 1947 and grew up on a farm in North Canterbury. He studied English and Politics at the Universities of Canterbury and Toronto. He teaches ESL in Auckland but retreats regularly with his wife and son to their farm in the Far North. He has published poetry and book reviews, mainly in the *Listener*.

Virginia Were lives in Devonport, on Auckland's North Shore. She was a member of the band Marie and the Atom. Her work has appeared in literary journals in New Zealand and Australia, and she won the PEN Best First Book Poetry Award for her collection, *Juliet Bravo Juliet*. She is currently completing her second book, which contains poetry and prose.

Judith White was born in Wellington and educated in Hastings. She worked as a laboratory technician, then travelled nomadically for five years. She won the Katherine Mansfield Short Story Centenary Award, which led to the publication of her story collection, *Visiting Ghosts*, in 1991, and twice won the *Sunday Star* short story competition. She now lives with her family in Auckland.

Steve Whitehouse was born in England at the tail end of World War II and was raised and educated in Wellington. He attended Victoria University and was involved in stage drama and television before moving overseas in the late 1960s. He now lives in New York, where he is a film-maker for the United Nations, and claims to be the only former sports editor of the VUW paper, *Salient*, to have met Kim Il Sung.

Amelia Wichman was born in 1974 in Hamilton and grew up in Auckland. She attended Auckland Girls' Grammar, Selwyn College and the University of Auckland, graduating BA in Human Sciences. She is currently living in Melbourne, where she is studying social work. *Nemesis* is her first published work.

Wensley Willcox was born in Christchurch and educated at Canterbury University. Her published work includes *Headlands* (1997), a collection of poetry with six other women, and a book of 'faction', *Poorman Oranges* (1987). Married for forty years, she has lived and worked in Auckland since 1969.

Frith Williams was born in 1972 in Christchurch and named after the girl next door. When not overseas on a bicycle she lives at Paekakariki Beach. She took Bill Manhire's writing course, won the McMillan Brown prize for Writers and has been published in California and in the *'Top of the Morning' Book of Incredibly Short Stories.*

Alison Wong was born in Hastings in 1960. She is a BSc in mathematics and a graduate of the creative writing courses at Victoria University and Whitireira Community Polytechnic. Her poetry has appeared in *Takahe*, *Printout* and *Mutes & Earthquakes*. She has spent several years in China and now lives in Titahi Bay with her husband and young son. She is currently working on a novel.

Louise Wrightson is a 48-year-old bookseller and writer who lives in Wilton, Wellington. Since completing Bill Manhire's Creative Writing Course at Victoria in 1996 she has had poetry and prose published in *Sport*, *Metro* and *Landfall* and in 1997 she won the New Zealand Poetry Society's International Poetry Competition.